WAYLAID

ED LIN

WAYLAID

KAYA PRESS

A Moebius strip of love and respect to Cindy, Doris, Dan, Alice, George and Cindy; nothing feels better than blood on blood. This book wouldn't be alive without the care of Sunyoung, Julie, Jae Hee, Thai, Melinda and Jackie. Ricola-sized shoutouts to Grace, Gary, Gayle, Darrell, Carla, Parag, Nhan, Gita, Katherine, Ed, Joe, Howard, Dan, Steve, Bennett and Mad Alex. The sun never sets on our backs: Kaya, AAJA, SAJA, AAWW, AAI, Peeling the Banana, Something to Say, Yellow Rage, A2BC, AAAA, 2G, CSWA, SAYA! and Uncle Teddy Happy.

Published by Kaya Press, an imprint of Muae Publishing
P.O. Box 7492
New York, NY 10116
www.kaya.com

Book design by Thai Nguyen

Manufactured in Canada

Distributed by D.A.P./Distributed Art Publishers
155 Avenue of the Americas, 2nd Floor
New York, NY 10013
(800) 338-BOOK www.artbook.com

ISBN 1-885030-32-0
Library of Congress Catalog Card Number: 2002104009

State of the Arts

NYSCA

This publication is made possible with public funds from the New York State Council on the Arts, a state agency, as well as the JPMorgan Chase SMARTS Regrant Program and the Asian American Arts Alliance, the Lower Manhattan Cultural Council, Soo Kyung Kim, Wook Hun and Sun Hee Koo, Eileen Tabios, Ronald and Susan Yanagihara, and many others.

for Charlie

CHAPTER 1

I was about 12 years old when I knew I had to get laid soon. No more of this jerking off. That was for fags.

The idea had been put into my head by Vincent, a Benny from Brooklyn. Bennys were young whites who came down to our hotel in the summers to pollute New Jersey's shores. They didn't go to college and worked in factories or as secretaries. All of them were from Bayonne, Elizabeth, Newark or New York, hence the name.

Vincent and I were sitting on the office couch playing Warlords when he turned to me and asked, "You gotten laid yet?"

"Nah. Not yet."

"Well, why not? You're like 11, right?"

"I'm 12," I said, straightening my back.

"Yeah, whatever, you should get laid. Girls were all over me when I was like eight. I was all over them, too." Vincent scratched his right side and his nipples visibly hardened. I never saw him with a shirt on, but he never shivered when he slipped into the frigid air of the office, wearing only a pair of tight black trunks and aquarium blue flip flops.

I had on a New Orleans Mardi Gras t-shirt that I'd found in one of the rooms and a pair of Yankees shorts. Imitation leather slippers from Taiwan left treads on the top of my feet where the straps crisscrossed.

"What for, Vincent?"

"'What for?' What the fuck kind of question is that?" He punched playfully at my arm. "What for! For getting your dick wet!"

I hit the reset button on the Atari and starting pounding away at Vincent's warlord.

"Hey hey hey!" he yelped as he fumbled to pull up the controller, which had slipped out of his hands and into his crotch.

This was Vincent's fourth straight weekend at our hotel. Vincent always wanted Room 59, because he was born that year and because it was close to the pool. It was also far from the office, which was important because he was sneaking in his two cousins with his girlfriend so he could pay the two-person rate instead of the four-person rate, which was 10 bucks more. Vincent told me because we were friends and we had an understanding between us.

Vincent was in his early 20s, with a face that was long and narrow like a skinny tree trunk. His thick black hair was cropped short and stood straight up, like magnified photos of stubble before the razor cuts the chin clean. He was "Vincent," never "Vinny," because Vinny was the name of some pizza joint in New York, and it wasn't the real Italian pizza, anyway. You needed a fork and a knife to eat real pizza. Real Italian pizza was thicker and had more stuff in it. Vincent had never had real Italian pizza, but that was the first thing he was going to do when he got to Italy, where his grandfather was from. Vincent was working at some construction job his uncle got him, but at night he was studying to be a cop. He was going to take me to Coney Island in his squad car one day. We were going to ride the Cyclone and eat hot dogs.

I had moved the Atari and the television into the office because it got so busy during the summertime that it didn't make sense to stay inside the living quarters and walk into and out of the office every five minutes for every BING! BING! BING! of the desk bell. Nobody hit that bell just once. Besides, it was June, and the temperature was cranking up. The office was air-conditioned and our living quarters weren't. It had to be that way because my parents said it wasn't worth air conditioning the living quarters. But if the office wasn't kept cold, customers would think the air conditioners in the rooms didn't work.

As a result, I spent a lot of time on the office couch. Vincent would drop in to hang out and play Atari with me when his girlfriend was pissed at him, which was usually a few hours on Saturday morning and a few more hours on Sunday morning.

I liked having someone to play games with. I was an only child, and my parents could never tell if I was playing Atari or watching television, even when blocky tanks, planes, or spaceships were firing at each other on the screen. They wouldn't have had time to play games even if they knew how. Friends, forget about it. No one wanted to hang out at our hotel. And it was too busy for me to ever leave for long enough to have friends outside of school.

"I'm going to win again!" I yelled.

I felt like such a loser when Vincent talked about girls. Vincent always talked about his fucking adventures – how he fucked his married neighbor who was 40 but was as tight as a 20-year-old, and how he fucked three sisters in three days and two of them were virgins. I preferred hearing his stories to having him ask me who I was fucking. I only had stories about me winning fights, which I did often enough because I was big for my age, but I knew I was letting him down.

"I know you kids are fucking in school. I know you are."

"I only heard about the two retarded kids, and I don't even think they meant it," I said.

Vincent laughed. "Retarded pussy! Shit, pussy's pussy, who cares," he said, taking his hands off the Atari controller. "You gotta like someone in school. I know you do. Some girls already start developing, you know? Their asses kinda turn out like fenders, and the headlights, you know they're going on high beam." His warlord flickered and died. Defeat was drawn out in crude, blinking video blocks. "Some little oriental girl? You been keeping her a secret? You give her some bamboo? You slip it to her?"

"Naw, I'm the only one in my school. Anyway, Chinese girls are ugly. I like blondes. Or redheads if they don't have too many freckles." Vincent shook his head from side to side, keeping his pupils fixed on me.

"I've fucked Chinese girls. God-damned cute. I fucked one last week, that's why Patty's pissed at me. I just told her."

"Then why are you still with Patty? You could go out with someone different every weekend. She just gives you too much shit." I was thinking that when I was old enough, I would be fucking left and right because there were so many women wanting cock in the world. Maybe I was old enough now, since I was getting hard-ons all the time. If I found a dynamite bombshell, I'd make her my girlfriend. But Patty was no bombshell. She had huge tits, but her nose drooped down like the mascot on the Moosehead Beer label. I never told Vincent that.

"Why am I still going out with Patty? Because I love her. You know, I really do. I'm gonna marry her. We're gonna have kids and everything." His mouth narrowed into a scythe. "But she don't have no chain on my dick. I don't gotta pull in the leash until the ring's on the finger. Then we'll see."

I knew all about the powerful drive of horniness from reading the letters in the issues of *Penthouse* and *Swank* I'd find cleaning rooms, but never having had sex lent a certain mystique to it all, especially stuff like S&M or ass-fucking. It was like reading about being weightless in space; this one astronaut woke up to find a hand wrapped around his neck and tightening. But it turned out to be his own hand.

"I know this girl here who will suck your dick for 10 bucks. We used to take the same bus together. She don't fuck, but you can come on her tits, she don't care. Her name's Chris or Karen and she's in Room 30," said Vincent. He threw his head back like a horse tossing its mane. "I know you've got at least 10 bucks."

I saw the girl in Room 30. She couldn't ever get me hard.

He traced my look of skepticism with his eyes and drew the wrong conclusion.

"No, it's okay. She doesn't care about you orientals." His hands on his thighs flipped to open palms.

I felt a pin slip into my stomach. Vincent's a friend, I told myself, he doesn't mean anything.

I hit reset on the Atari and the game began again.

"Hey, c'mon now! That's not fair!" Vincent put up a fight for a few seconds, then tossed his controller onto the couch next to me.

"So anyway, you have to get laid," he said, running a single finger through his hair. Vincent looked at the office clock, which was a large plastic-molded Marlboro sign with a dial in the middle of the second "o." A cowboy in spurs leaned against the "M." It was a quarter to 11.

Vincent got up and stretched, cracking bones in his lower back. "Maybe Patty's cooled off by now. Remember what I told you. I'll be disappointed if you don't get laid by the end of the summer. Real fucking disappointed." He wagged a finger at me and pulled at his waistband. "Or maybe you'll turn queer on me or something. Maybe you're fag bait already!"

Right then, Peter Fiorello walked into the office with Mrs. Fiorello. The Fiorellos were the first regulars I'd met – they were both retired, and they'd been coming down to our place since we'd bought it. Each of them kissed Vincent on the cheek. They were old enough to be Vincent's parents, maybe even his grandparents. The three of them together smiling in a semi-embrace looked like a spaghetti-sauce commercial. The only things missing were the aprons and wooden spoons.

Peter Fiorello's shrunken patch of short white hair looked like a knit cap. Peter would walk around shirtless in the summer, exposing old tattoos on his chest and arms that were blue and blurred beyond recognition. His tits were smeared excess red and brown paint, and they clung to his chest like dried mud. Peter wore a gold chain with a religious pendant on it and dark shades. I never saw him with his shades off or without a smelly, smoldering cigar in his hand. He smiled often, flashing two rows of rotten corn kernels.

Mrs. Fiorello was loud, large, and annoying. She had big pouffy hair with plump breasts and a stomach to match. Her skin was covered with impossibly dense freckles. There must have been a thousand dark brown dots per square inch all over the massive surface area of her body. Seeing her in a one-piece bathing suit that didn't even show that much skin took away my faith in God.

The Fiorellos were the hotel's only steady customers throughout the four seasons. They lived somewhere in New York, but there were too many loud blacks and Puerto Ricans up there. They wanted to come to our hotel at the Jersey shore where they could relax and talk to us nice Chinese people.

"Watch this man. He's going places," Peter said, wrapping an arm around Vincent's waist and stroking Vincent's neck with his free hand. He liked Vincent and would touch him so much it was worrisome.

"Peter, you tell the boy to listen to what I say, okay?" said Vincent, making a meaningless gesture at me with his right hand.

"You listen to Vincent, he's going to be on top. He's the man to look out for," Peter said.

"Vincent is a good boy. If you turn out like him, your mother will be really proud," said Mrs. Fiorello. Vincent winked, extracted himself, and walked around the Fiorellos. His slippers made sucking sounds as he walked back to Room 59.

"I used to look like that," said Peter, standing at the office window. He leaned back and rubbed the scraggly white fuzz on his chest.

"Now you're twice the man, Peter," said Mrs. Fiorello, patting his stomach.

"You see this? You see this? Always a compliment with a nit-pick. Always a slap with a kiss." He tapped his cigar and his nose twitched as he winked from behind his impenetrable shades, which were as dark as a wet blackboard.

"Oh, stop, Peter!" said Mrs. Fiorello, taking a playful swat at his face.

Listening to the Fiorellos talk was like watching an old stand-up routine, complete with elbowing and winks:

"These cigars really aren't bad for you," he might start.

"Peter never inhales. He only breathes out, so it's okay."

"You know, she'll be the death of me, not these things. Cigars are a habit you can break, but women always break you first."

"Peter doesn't need to be broken. All those years of being in the Navy broke you. He cleans so much around the house, I feel like I'm the one making a mess. I just watch the television and put my feet up."

"She puts her feet up on my back when I'm scrubbing the floors. It's abuse, I tell ya. You people know how to treat your women. Put them in their place in China."

"Peter!"

"It's true, they can't even walk next to their husbands, they have to walk behind them."

"They have such pretty dresses, the Chinese women. Doesn't your mother have any like that? She should wear them. Pretty and silk."

The Fiorellos would always throw in something about China or Chinese food, as if I couldn't follow a conversation if they didn't. Mrs. Fiorello turned to the television screen. "This is a computer game, right? You shouldn't play them anymore, they rot your brain. I read it in *Newsweek*."

"They develop motor skills and improve hand-eye coordination," I said, using my prepared answer from the video-game magazines. "They also keep kids off the street and out of trouble. Video games don't require parental supervision, unlike many movies, and nobody gets hurt playing them. They're also good for children who don't have any playmates."

Mrs. Fiorello rolled her eyes and dropped to the couch

next to me. I felt the creaky frame give a little and the seat cushion grew tight. "You think you're so smart. Just wait until it's too late," she said. After a heavy sigh, she added, "Is your mother in?"

"Hold on a sec," I said. I turned off the Atari and walked back into the living quarters. I went into my parents' bedroom and shook my mother awake. It was 11 now, about time for her to get up, anyway. I could tell by the motel's log that she'd been up until five renting rooms, but six hours of sleep was more than enough. Today was going to be another busy day for the hotel, and there were rooms we needed to clean. In a few minutes, my mother was fully dressed and in the office. I heard an exaggerated but brief greeting exchanged amongst the three of them.

I shut the door to the office, feeling the heat of the living quarters. I followed the worn path on the living-room rug, between a lopsided couch and a bare TV stand, back to my room. Talking to Vincent had made me think about this girl from school I liked, Lee Anderson. She had blonde hair and green eyes and was so cute, I couldn't help but look away when she caught me staring, which was about every two minutes. Even though she was just 12 like me, I could tell that Lee was going to be a perfect girl when she grew up. She was already past a B cup, and she had long soft blonde hair that curled at her shoulders. Her body was growing in all the right places, and she was looking pretty damn sexy.

When we were in fourth grade together, she'd drunk beer from her Thermos and couldn't wake up after nap time. Maybe things would go easier for me if I got her drunk again. Beer could make a lot of things possible.

But I got the feeling she liked me, too. Maybe she had a speck of dust in her eye the day I thought she winked at me. So what if it was. She was definitely going to be mine. I felt warm each time Lee smiled or said my name. She'd probably let me get into her pants sober. Get my dick wet.

I pulled out my Monopoly set and took an issue of *Cheri* from under the game board. I reread the letters. Women driving, walking, or sitting alone were dying to get naked and suck and fuck.

Some mornings I woke up with my own hand wrapped around my cock.

CHAPTER 2

The hotel had been beautiful once, back in the 1950s.

I knew because I'd found a box of old color pamphlets in the crawlspace that ran under the complete length of the hotel. The pictures were in soft, faded colors – the blues were baby blues and the reds were pink. Flying wooden ramparts painted gleaming white connected the tips of the two parallel wings of the hotel like a big suspension bridge. Voluptuous cars iced with chrome looked like they could have driven out of Arnold's parking lot on "Happy Days." Men wore suits and hats, and women had scarves and gloves.

Three decades went by. It was the 1980s.

The ramparts were now rotting in stacks in the thickly wooded area that pressed up against the outside of the even- and odd-numbered wings. The hotel was laid out like the letter U with the office at the bottom. An asphalt driveway ran the entire inside length of the letter, from the four-lane interstate highway that lead to the beaches to the office and then back.

The big cars had been replaced by beat-up Datsuns and Thunderbirds that crawled around the parking lot like insects with a leg or wing torn off.

Men had ditched their suits and hats and women, their scarves and gloves. Now everyone wore a unisex uniform of t-shirts and jeans, or bathing suits and cut-offs in the summer. Their faces were desperate for sex, for love, for another smoke; men with a few days of stubble, women with uneven layers of makeup. Their hard eyes and harder mouths would only loosen up with booze or some pot.

I don't remember much of life before the hotel. I was born in New York City, but we'd moved out to the Jersey shore and bought the place when I was eight. The sellers were a white couple with a son about my age.

I remember racing slot-cars with that other little boy while our parents talked about the details of the sale. The hand-held controllers smelled like blown-out birthday candles as they heated up. If you didn't let off on the trigger on the turn, the car would fishtail and flip off the track. Our parents were talking in the kitchen with the door closed. I couldn't hear what they were saying as the cars whined around and around, but I could see them through the plate glass window. My father was standing at the dining table, sleeves rolled up. He was slightly shorter than my mother, with a ruddy complexion that made him look like he was drunk or really mad, but he was never in either of those states. He had curly black hair, which was a little unusual, but his eyes and wide cheeks tagged him as Chinese. He was poring over the blueprints of the hotel, examining the structure and soundness of the plan and figuring out how salvageable the hotel was in its current state of disrepair. Was that when my parents hammered out the details of renting out rooms to hookers and johns?

The main reason why my father had wanted the hotel was because he wanted to have his own business. Like all his classmates from Taiwan who had come to the U.S., he had been passed over for promotions at the civil-engineering company he'd been working at. His boss had told him his English wasn't good enough, but after a few months with some text books, my father found out that none of the engineers, including his boss, really knew proper spelling or grammar. He ended up making a lot of corrections in the firm's reports. My mother told me they'd given him a bottle of champagne when he left, which he poured out in the street before throwing the bottle into the gutter.

After we moved into the hotel, my father was usually covered with rust or flakes of rotted wood. There were burn holes in his pants, holes that corresponded to scars on his skin. He'd slip into the crawlspace because of a leaking pipe or a sinking bathroom floor and solder and nail away, surfacing only for food before heading back down. I would join him down there sometimes, but my main job was handling the front desk. My father never wanted to deal with customers. Unlike my mother, he was embarrassed about his English, though his was much better than hers.

When the hotel filled up in the summer, we could just lock the office door and put the closed sign in the window. When the fall arrived, we had to scrounge for business. We needed to keep the office open and unlocked to get all the business we could.

The bulk of the business during those times was the three-hour rental.

On the weekends, during the school year, my mother would lay down a folded comforter behind the counter for me and set an alarm clock by the bell. She would leave the office light on, telling me to turn my head and close my eyes, and it wouldn't keep me up. Late nights were prime john time, and if the light was out, they might think the place was closed and go to another hotel or use our parking space. My mother was too tired from watching the office the whole week while I was in school and needed to catch up on sleep on the weekends. As a woman, I'm sure she also didn't relish the thought of being in the same room as the cock side of the money equation.

Sometimes I just couldn't sleep, even if no one came all night. When that happened, I would read the letters sections of sex magazines, which I could easily hide in the folds of the comforter when I heard a customer coming in.

I first saw the letters in an issue of *Hustler* I found cleaning rooms when I was about seven. When I was with my mom, she'd throw out all the porn right off the bat, making sure to rip it up in front of me. But that time I found it under the bed and shoved it under my shirt before she saw.

That magazine had an article on how to find hotels

that charged hourly rates. It recommended going to non-chain hotels close to train stations. Or you could pick up hookers by the train stations late at night and they would know which hotels to go to. A fuckhole wasn't only a cunt; it was also a place to hole up and fuck. Like our hotel. After reading the article, I wondered how much it would cost for me to get laid with a hooker, and how much money was in the cash drawer.

When I was 10, a john I was renting a room to told me he was picking up girls by the New Jersey Transit station in nearby Asbury Park. The prostitutes wore short skirts and long coats and carried open umbrellas.

After all my years at the hotel, I'd never seen any hookers – not their full bodies anyway. They wouldn't prance around the parking lot afterwards, trying to pick up more tricks. The most I ever saw was a dim face between the dashboard and sunblind of a car pulled up outside the office. Sometimes they'd be smoking or fixing their makeup.

The john told me they were $20, $5 extra to fuck them up the ass and $5 more for swallowing. So a room and a no-frills prostitute were $40 in total.

"It's worth it to get laid, isn't it?" he asked, as he filled out a registration card, moving as fast as he could make up the information. He was wearing a dark brown corduroy jacket, a grimy button-down shirt, and dark slacks. Silvery hair cascaded into the gap between his lobster-red neck and his loosened collar. He looked like he was about 50.

"Are they pretty?" I asked. He laughed.

"I'm not looking for Miss America, but they're pretty for black girls. The white ones are kind of ugly."

"How good is it?"

"How good is it? It's great. It's like following through on a good clean punch."

"What does it feel like?"

"What does it feel like…" He was smiling. "Look, kid, just give me the goddamn key."

I fell asleep once with the fifth anniversary issue of *Celebrity Skin* over my face and didn't hear the alarm go off. It was a lot softer than a BING! The clock alarm went on for so long, my mother got up and came into the office. I hadn't fully awoken when she swatted my face with the rolled-up magazine.

"You go to hell, you look at these pictures!" she screamed, kicking at my shoulders as I scrambled to my feet.

"I was just reading the letters!"

"You go to hell! Where did you get this from!?!?"

"I got it from cleaning the hotel rooms!"

"You don't touch this anymore! You go to hell!" She never said anything more about porn mags, and I continued to add to my collection. But from that day on, I would bring only my school books to read at night, leaving the magazines in my room. That way, she wouldn't have to see it.

I once asked my mother why anybody would want to rent one of our hotel rooms for just three hours.

"They tire from driving," she said. "They want lie

down and take little nap." We were distant enough to let that howling wind of a lie exist between our worlds. And it let me know it was okay to lie to her, too.

Late Friday was big for hourly rentals. The husbands could always say they were trying to finish up some work at the office before the weekend.

At one in the morning, there were about a dozen rooms that had to be cleaned to be rented out again.

I yawned and rubbed my eyes before picking up a plastic bucket in each hand and followed my mother out the office door. She held a bundle of folded sheets, pillowcases, and towels. My mother had a mop of straight black hair that dangled down to her shoulders. As we walked along the curved part of the U-shaped driveway, the light from the outdoor spotlights reflected in the smooth crescents of her hair.

When we got to 11A, my mother knocked on the door to make sure the occupants had left.

Once upon a time, 11A had been 13, but then it had been changed so the rooms on the odd-numbered wing went from 11 to 11A and then to 15. Nobody wanted to rent a room 13. Like they wouldn't get lucky or something if they did.

My mother opened the lock with the master key and turned to look at me.

"You have everything, right?" she asked. I nodded and shook the buckets.

One of my buckets held spray bottles filled with bathroom cleaners, air fresheners, and rug cleaners. A worn toilet-bowl brush dangled over the side of the bucket, the bristles pressed flat against the battered wire rim.

My other bucket was packed with soap, rolls of toilet paper, and sheaves of sanitary labels. The soap bars were slender white rectangles embossed with "THANK YOU" on one side, like we were thanking our customers for taking a shower and trying to be clean. The soap lathered up about as well as a Lego block and would break into pieces if you tried to use it more than once. Our toilet paper was so thin, you'd feed fingers up your ass.

Each hotel room was basically the same except that some of the black-and-white televisions had rabbit-ear antennas and some had inverted wire coat hangers. They all had a simple desk, a night stand, and a chair made of pressed wood. Push on any of the furniture the wrong way and it would splinter apart. There were burn marks on the desks and night stands, even though each room had chipped-glass ashtrays. The two windows had shades as heavy as burlap. When they were closed, they blocked out sound and light and the view of the parking lot.

The beds consisted of flimsy metal frames and creaky box springs with broken slats of wood topped with a doughy mattress. Two limp pillows slouched against the pressed-wood headboard. Some of the headboards had stickers on them with instructions on how to operate the vibrating motor for a quarter, but the motion devices had been ripped out and thrown away long before we'd owned the place. The wall-to-wall carpeting looked like every marching band in the country had dragged flour sacks of grime across it. Every color in the carpet had been corrupted into a different shade of dark green.

The bathroom tile wasn't much better, but at least we provided soap and clean towels. We weren't classy enough to have vials of shampoo because we ordered from the economy section of our supplier catalog. Only the standard and luxury sections had shampoo.

I sat on the edge of the bathtub and scrubbed at the gunk in the shower with the toilet brush, shaking a can of some no-name imitation of Ajax so that it snowed into the scummy tub. I scrubbed again.

I looked at myself in the bathroom mirror. My hair was straight like my mother's, but about twice as thick. It stuck out sideways at odd angles like clumps of crab grass. My eyes were bloodshot and my face looked old and tired.

I finished with the toilet and slipped a paper label around the folded rim and seat cover. I shook the toilet brush into the sink, then scrubbed it against the edges of the sink and the faucet handles.

My mother had been stripping the sheets off the bed. When she stopped, I turned to see what was the matter. She was looking at a dark spot on the mattress and frowning.

"We have to flip this one," she said, nodding her head towards the stain in the other lower corner. I pulled at the seam of the fabric until I could get a good hold on the thick, mushy mattress, then helped her wrestle it off of the crooked bed frame. Most of the mattresses and bed frames were from a demolition company that would strip everything out of a house before pulverizing it.

Soon the mattress was turned upside down and pushed back into place. There were dark brown stains — all near the same area as the wet one — on this side of the mattress, too. Some were oval-shaped, some looked like warped coffee-cup stains, and others looked like little amoebae with several pseudopodia. They were dry, though, and that was all that was important. My mother unfurled the new sheets and threw them on top.

The wet comestains were now on the underside of the mattress.

CHAPTER 3

I drew an X on June 1 in green magic marker. Another day over. Two more weeks until school was finished. The calendar was stuck on my wall with a plastic green push-pin. Each month featured a different field of flowers with, "THANK YOU, Amboy Linen Services Inc.," printed in off-white across the bottom of the picture. Tulips in April. Roses in November. June had daffodils.

A calendar I kept in my Erector set box also had daffodils for June, but they were strewn across the stomach of a naked brunette, her legs spread and ending in two spiked heels that looked like they would snap in two if she tried standing. Luckily, she was lying down in the back seat of a Cadillac on what looked like a really sunny day. I lay back in my bed and drew my knees up. I balanced the centerfold calendar against my thighs and dropped both hands under the waistband of my briefs.

I caressed, kneaded, and pulled. I could feel some tautness in the skin, but I could tell I wouldn't be able to come this time. As soon as that thought entered my mind, the stiffness melted away, leaving my cock small and limp. I could keep rubbing and stroking, but it wouldn't do any good. Once, I was so desperate and had tugged so hard, that it started bleeding, leaving me with a chain of tiny scabs on my cock for a week.

Sometimes it was easier to come if I used a picture from the hard-core magazines, which were printed on heavy stock. Those girls liked it when you came in their mouths or on their tits. But they didn't look very pretty, not as pretty as *Playboy* or *Penthouse* girls. They had tiny scars on their necks or chests and lines around their wide-open mouths and eyes. Acne on their body. The soft-core magazines had better looking girls – with makeup, pretty smiles, painted nails – but they wouldn't do too much outside of posing. They wouldn't even finger themselves.

It was important to jerk off. Vincent told me you had to jerk off before every date because if you didn't, you would come early and the girl would get pissed off.

That was bad. I saw enough ads for stay-hard creams to know that coming early was embarrassing, even worse than not being able to get it up, since if you couldn't get hard, the girl wasn't sexy or wasn't doing enough. I was never limp when I saw a centerfold.

Jerking off helped build up dick control. If you were good, you could ball about a half hour. Then if she was sexy enough, you could get hard again a few minutes later. How many times did the johns get to come in three hours?

I wanted to get good at masturbating, but I could only do it about three or four times a week at most. I kept a pack of towelettes and Burger King napkins under my bed.

There would be nothing to clean up today, though. The

skin felt a little raw, so I withdrew my hands and turned on my side, the centerfold calendar slipping off the bed.

A tiny rattling sound at the ledge by my window caught my attention. It was the radiometer, a solar toy I'd bought on my fourth-grade class field trip to Thomas Edison's lab. Everything in the lab had been preserved exactly the way he'd left it when he died. A giant dried-out elephant ear hung from one of the lab's walls. It looked like a fun place, one where you could make something new instead of just fixing broken things again and again. It didn't look anything like my father's base-ment workshop. The gift shop had been right next to the lab, and I'd used eight quarters I'd slipped from the soda machine's change box to buy the radiometer.

The toy was made up of four diamond-shaped panels suspended on a wire and looked like a miniature weather vane sealed in a glass bulb. One side of each panel was painted white, and the other side was painted black. When sunlight hit it, the device spun because the light reflected off the white side of the panel and was absorbed by the black side. The black surface warmed up more than the white one, and since gas molecules recoil faster from the hot surface, the vane would spin. The brighter the light, the faster it would go. In the early mornings, the toy would turn slowly, shakily. By the early afternoon, it spun furiously, making tick-tick-tick sounds as the radial vector of the axis grew and the toy scraped against the insides of the glass bulb.

I'd wanted a radiometer ever since seeing a picture of one in my science textbook. I liked reading that book, which had a solar eclipse on the cover, because it explained things. Why amputated frog legs jumped when hooked up to a battery. How a prism broke up white light into colors. Best of all were the chapters on the planets. Looking at the picture of the earth rising from the moon in the glossy-pictures section made me want to shoot up into space. I wanted to be an astronaut so bad, I sent away for some freeze-dried ice cream so I would know what the food was like. I sent a $20 bill from the cash register to mail order five rations, but I never got anything.

I didn't want to be anything else. Not a policeman, not a fireman. I wanted to go out into orbit. I figured that by the time I was old enough to join NASA, we'd probably already have space travel.

Being out there, it would always be night, there'd be beautiful lights all around, and I would know the peace and serenity of heaven. But my dreams of floating weightless were always interrupted by the BING! BING! BING! That little bell going off put your life on hold. You heard it and you hopped to it. It didn't matter if you were eating, sleeping, reading, or shitting. "BING!" and you'd open that door and smile and say, "Can I help you?"

Then I realized that here I was thinking about what I was going to do when I was all grown-up, and I hadn't even fucked anybody yet.

I was one of the smartest kids in school because I was forced to grow up in a business environment. I made change. I read the newspapers in the office, and when I finished those, there was nothing else to read but my science or my literature textbooks. I also handled credit-card transactions, which were a pain.

First, I had to look up the card number in a booklet issued monthly to make sure it wasn't reported stolen or missing. The booklet was about a quarter of an inch thick with pages as thin as onion skins. Then I had to call in the card information and the transaction fee. The operator would read a 10-digit authorization number, which I had to write on the slip. I never had to deal with a stolen card, but a lot of cards were rejected for non-payment. I had to tell people I couldn't rent rooms to them as I tore the slips up in their faces. It was a good thing that I was a fairly big kid.

Other kids looked up to me because I could put on my front-desk demeanor and assert authority. Also, I was five feet eight inches and 120 pounds in seventh grade. I couldn't stay after school for stuff like spelling bees or wrestling practice, though. My mother would be tired from watching the office the whole day, and I would have to take over for her. Anything else I wanted to do I had to get done during school hours.

I had friends in school, but a lot of kids were nice to me because they thought I could get them a room to party in. I'd get invited to go drinking in the woods, but there was no way I could go. I had to stay in on weekend nights to meet johns and clean their rooms after they checked out. Besides, my parents wouldn't want me out drinking.

When I was really young, I went to a kid's birthday

party. His mother looked at me funny as I walked into their house. She decided to move the party to the porch outside, even though the wooden-plank furniture was still a little wet from the rain the day before. She was so nice to me, I was getting more attention than the birthday boy. She walked me to and from the bathroom. It made me feel real strange, and after the party, I never talked to that kid again.

Astronauts didn't need friends or family, anyway. I liked to ride my Huffy around the hotel and pretend I was heading for deep space. A small stretch of asphalt connected the ends of the driveway near the highway on the inside of the U, completing an oval track. As I did lap after lap, I would try to run over every stray pebble, pretending they were asteroids I had to destroy. Clockwise and then counter-clockwise. Twenty-five laps one way, 25 the other. I would pedal faster and faster, trying to reach escape velocity so I could break out of the orbit of life at the hotel and into a better world. One with sex but with no BING! BING! BING! or Bennys or johns.

Just one week before the end of school, I found a note on my chair that said, "FUCKIN CHINKS GO BACK TO CHINA!" I smiled and sat down. Three boys – Ray Millar, Chris Cohen, and Robbie Malone – grinned and nodded to each other.

Ray was a bony kid with uneven sheaves of black hair. His frequent smiles showed filthy braces. Chris, who was called "Crispy" because of the fried, bubbly texture of his acne-ridden face, was on the fatter side of chubby and wore his hair in a crew cut because he thought bangs caused pimples. Robbie was skinny like Ray and looked meaner. Not in a menacing way, but like the underfed caged lab rat at the back of the classroom.

I felt around inside my desk for my ruler, the one with the metal rim from my father's workshop. I slipped it into the sleeve of my shirt. As we filed out for gym class, I cupped my right hand to keep the ruler up my sleeve. I saw that orange cones and hard rubber balls had been set up in the gym as we walked to the girls' and boys' locker rooms. Dodge ball again.

I sat down on the scarred, splintered locker-room bench and watched Crispy. He was the biggest of the three. If I came at him, I knew Ray and Robbie would back off. I was right. As I came up to Crispy, hands at my sides, those skinny white boys slipped away like dogs at the sound of a newspaper rolling up. Crispy saw me but played it cool, working on his combination lock. He looked at me from the corner of his eye, spinning the dial to the right, six, seven, then eight times.

"That was a nice note you left on my desk," I said quietly. Crispy turned his head, keeping his hand on the lock.

"What are you talking about?" he asked with a smile. I shook the ruler free from my sleeve and swung the metal edge down onto his hand. He screamed like a girl, delicately holding his limp, bleeding hand like a carefully arranged bouquet. I brought up my foot and planted my Puma into his stomach, aiming for lunch. When he dropped to his knees and puked, I saw that I'd hit breakfast, too.

On the last day of school, my seventh-grade teacher Miss Creach called me up to the front of the class. I'd gotten the top report card. She gave me a hug and a t-shirt printed with a picture of a German Shepherd. "Top Dog" was written on the back. Miss Creach was young, about 25, and had a really pretty face, eyes, and hair, like Agent 99 on "Get Smart." She was kinda skinny with nice legs that she liked to unveil with a tug on her skirt when she sat down. Her ass seemed to have the right plumpness, too. But her tits were too small. That was the only thing wrong with her. That wouldn't stop some guys, though. There were a lot of letters in the magazines from fans of that.

"And second place is Lee Anderson," said Miss Creach. From my seat I stared at Lee Anderson's ass as she went up to the front. She got a hug and a book of certificates for free French fries at McDonald's.

When she walked by to go back to her seat, I held up the t-shirt and said, "Lee, I'll trade ya!"

"No way!" she called back, smiling.

As I turned back to the front I saw that Miss Creach was frowning at me.

Now that summer vacation had arrived, the walkers lingered around the parking lot before going home. That let them hang out a little longer with the kids who had to wait for buses. Because of family vacations, a lot of friends wouldn't see each other the entire summer.

Walkers were kids who lived so close to school, they didn't have to ride buses. My stop was one of the farthest from the school, so I was never a walker. I never had family vacations, either.

Boys from the intermediate school across the street had come by to check up on the tit growth of my classmates. The burnouts smoked cigarettes and wore cut-off denim jackets with "Black Sabbath" or "Led Zeppelin" painted on the back. They were also on the hunt for fags. They'd taunted and punched the smaller boys all year, and today was their last chance until next year.

Crispy huddled by me. He'd given me three hard-core magazines to not kick his ass anymore.

"Regina Garrison is giving blow jobs under the bleachers by the soccer field," he said.

"Fucking bullshit," I said.

"She doesn't care if people watch," Crispy said.

Suddenly there were five intermediate-school kids surrounding us.

"There's a fucking faggot right here!" yelled a tall, skinny burnout, pointing to Crispy. There were so many of them, I didn't know what to do, so I stuck my hands in my pockets. Crispy dropped his bag and froze, then went limp in an act of self defense.

"Your dad got my dad fired!" yelled one of the burnouts. "You're so dead, little faggot!"

They grabbed Crispy's arms. In my head, I was yelling for him to kick them, but Crispy just tried to ball himself up.

Now I understood how someone could just stand aside and watch their friend get beaten up. It wasn't that we were outnumbered, but when you see someone give up and not even try to fight, you wonder why you should. Why stick up for someone who won't even fight for himself?

"You're not even going to punch me, you little girl?" taunted the burnout. "I think it's time to recycle you." He got two other intermediate kids, and they picked Crispy up by the legs. Crispy wriggled and screamed. They opened the lid to the garbage can and pumped him down headfirst into the trash. I heard Crispy's head banging on the sides of the can.

Then they pulled him out and dumped him in a bush. I could hear Crispy crying. His face was cut and bleeding, though it didn't look much worse than with the pimples alone.

"Hey, over here!" yelled a burnout about my size. He was pointing at me. "C'mon, you slanted cunt!" he shouted.

I pulled out a screwdriver from my back pocket.

"Shit, are you fucking crazy?" he asked, backing up. I didn't say anything. "Fucking psycho Bruce Lee. Go back to that fucking chinky hotel. You're crazy!"

After they left, I picked up Crispy's bag and helped him up. Crispy was still crying. We walked to the buses, stepping over crushed cigarette butts littering the lawn. It reminded me of all the trash I swept up when the Bennys were back at the hotel in full force. I could tell that for all their posturing, the burnouts were still novices at smoking. The butts weren't sucked down to the filter the way people at the hotel would do it.

"What the hell are you kids doing!" yelled Mrs.

Krackowski. Her bus was idling at the curb and she was standing at the top of the boarding steps with the door open. She was only about five feet tall, but she was as tough as cold biscuits. A huge pair of shades obscured most of her face.

"They just beat him up!" I yelled back. Crispy kept crying and wiping his bloody face.

"Just get him in here, and let's go! You're holding everybody up!" Mrs. Krackowski spat out. "This is one hell of a way to end your last day of school!"

CHAPTER 4

Renting out rooms to johns was just one part of the business. It was reliable income throughout the year, especially in the winter when there weren't many real customers. It paid for the groceries. I knew because it was me who went to the supermarket.

Business peaked from Memorial Day through Labor Day, when the Bennys would come down and party. The johns hated it when the Bennys came in because the room prices went up to $50 a night, with no special fuck-only rates.

The Bennys liked our hotel because it was near the beach. Rooms at that time of year were in pretty high demand, even with the increased rate. The Bennys made sure they got their money's worth. They'd pack in all their friends and have maybe eight people staying in a room: two on each bed; one on the floor between the beds; two in the closet; and one in the bathroom.

High-school girls really went for Benny men. The girls would be out of school for the summer and looking for something more exciting than fast food and surfing. Cheese fries and Space Invaders had nothing on drinking and screwing under the boardwalk after hours.

Benny women were on the prowl for potential long-term boyfriend/husband material, but they were lucky if they had the same guy two nights in a row. I had to call taxis to take girls to the train stop after they got ditched at our hotel.

Business was fast and furious in the summer, and when it got to be two or three in the morning and there were no rooms left, people would get really desperate. The last thing they wanted was a drive back to the city without even getting a chance to score. They would beg for a room, a dirty room, or even a room with other people in it. People wanted to sleep in the office. Others were willing to pay twice the room rate and sometimes offered more than just cash.

Because of the Bennys, summers were no vacation for me. I had more work to do than when I was in school. More rooms to clean. More cigarettes, crushed cans, and broken glass to pick up around the hotel while avoiding the bees that had been attracted by the smell of alcohol. More drunk assholes to step around. I'd find used condoms and hotel blankets under the picnic tables all the time. Sometimes people would still be asleep, wrapped in the blankets.

They'd also mess up the pool, which was surrounded by an unraveling stretch of green plastic-coated chain link fence that had buckled and warped from Bennys pushing each other against it or running their car fenders into it. If a supporting rod popped out of its joint, the fence would pucker and come apart. Sharp, rusted tips of cross-hatched wire stuck out from the plastic coating, looking like tire-shredders embedded in asphalt behind a "DO NOT ENTER" sign. One of my duties was to go around with a pair of pliers and thick wire and try to mend the fence, pulling it taut and tying it up.

Cracked concrete framed the swimming pool, which was close to the highway, between the tips of the U. You had to put your towel over the weather-beaten wooden pool furniture before you sat down, otherwise you'd get splinters. Most people used the bath towels from the hotel, and in the mornings, I would take the pole hook and pull out towels that had sunk to the bottom of the deep end and clogged up the drain. Sometimes I pulled out shorts and bikinis, too.

Bennys would often hop the fence and fuck in the shallow end at night. It was like joining the mile-high club or something. The Jacques Cousteau club, I guess. The water would still be warm because it retains heat in the evening better than the land. I learned that from my softcover science workbook. Water also made sex more buoyant and fluid. I learned that from letters to *Club International*.

In the hot sun, I got hard watching women lying on their chests, bikini tops untied and straps hanging off the sides like bright, multicolored shoelaces. Would their tits be pressed flat permanently if they stayed like that too long? Would there be lines across their nipples from the wood planks?

I went around the pool deck, sweeping up cigarette

butts and thin pieces of broken brown and green glass from Budweiser and Heineken bottles. I saw a crushed, empty box of Marlboros under the recliner of a woman asleep with her top untied. I got down on my knees and reached for the box, turning my head up to try to peek at her tits.

"Hey, what are you doing, kid?" someone yelled. I stuck my head up. It was Vincent, smiling and standing by the garden hose that was coiled up near the shallow end. The hose was for people to wash sand off their feet and only carried cold water. Very cold water. The nozzle was in Vincent's hand.

"This is how you do it!" he yelled, turning the faucet on full blast and pointing it at the woman. The nozzle wasn't focused, so he sprayed about 10 people with freezing pellets that smacked against the skin and hurt because they were so cold. Everyone screamed and jumped up, including two women who forgot that their tops were untied. They scampered for cover on the deck near the deep end, hands cupping their tits.

"You fucking asshole sonovabitch! Motherfucker! Cocksucker! 'Talian faggot piece of shit!" they screeched. One was a blonde, the other was a redhead. Vincent was doubled over with laughter, but he didn't turn the hose off. He held the nozzle between his legs and jerked it around, like he was pissing on everyone.

I searched for the two missing bikini tops but only found one, tangled up with a pair of sunglasses. Looking at the pattern, I was glad to see it was the blonde's. I stretched it out and felt at the insides of each cup, as if I could squeeze the nipples that were once there. I went up to her and handed it back. If it were a *Penthouse* letter, she would have given me a deep French kiss and led me back to her room for a blow job and a hard fuck.

Instead, she snatched her bikini top away and slapped me hard as she yelled, "Fucking little chink pervert!" She had rings on her fingers. I ran my tongue through my mouth to make sure all my teeth were still there. The mark on my face stung and my cheek was slick with a suntan lotion smear.

Afterwards, I was looking forward to sitting back on the office couch and playing Atari, but when I went into the office, I found my father already lying there. He was wearing jeans, a thin t-shirt, and socks. His eyes were closed.

"What's going on here?" I asked.

"Back hurt," he said, not opening his eyes. His arms were folded across his stomach.

"Shouldn't you go see a doctor? This keeps happening."

"No, don't need doctor. No big deal."

"Do you want more aspirin?"

"No, doesn't do anything. Just have to lie down more."

"Why don't you lie down on the living-room couch?"

"That couch broken and hurt my back. And too hot there. Nicer here."

"You're too cheap to turn on our air conditioner."

"You spend most of your time in office. I'm downstair in the basement with cool air. Mommy is out cleaning rooms. Why should I turn on air conditioner?"

I heaved a sigh and set up the Atari. In about a

minute, I was sitting on the office floor, playing Superman.

"Is that video game?" asked my father from the couch.

"Yeah," I said without turning around to look at him.

"What game is that?"

"Superman."

I heard him shift on the couch and clear his throat.

"Can you get me some water?" he asked.

After dinner, when most of the Bennys had left the pool for the bars, I jumped in and held myself underwater just to see what drowning was like.

It was dark, quiet, and nice for about 15 seconds. Then the urge to breathe began to pound in my head and chest like knocks against Death's chamber. Drowning had to be the worst way to go because you couldn't scream and your thoughts bounced around as your head was being squeezed by water pressure. I could imagine the ache you would feel tearing away at your insides until you died.

I came up for a breath and went down again.

CHAPTER 5

I sat in the office, playing Adventure on the Atari. I'd finished the game a zillion times before, but I was sick of Superman, and all the other cartridges required two players to be any fun.

A Benny walked in, a six-pack of bottles of beer in one hand and a cooler the size of a doghouse swaying in the other.

"The ice machine is between Room 2 and Room 4," I said, pointing to the left.

"I'm not looking for the ice machine," he said. "I need a bottle opener. Ya got one, pal?" He showed a fresh cut on his thumb. "I thought they were twist-offs," he said, mushing the tiny flap of skin against the second knuckle of his index finger.

I looked under the office desk and pawed through the lost and found. Some of my best stuff had been left by customers. A thick leather shaving bag that I kept foreign coins in. Two Billy Idol tapes. A fountain pen. Strings of studded or ribbed Venus beads that you were supposed to feed into a girl's pussy or asshole, or even your own asshole, according to the hard-core magazines. A cock ring.

I found a bottle opener with a white plastic handle that was melted by the heat coils of a hotplate. The metal ends were spotted with rust, although I could still make out the words "STAINLESS STEEL TAIWAN." I handed it over the counter to the man.

"Can I have this?" he asked.

"Yeah, someone's left it here since last winter," I said.

"Thanks, pal, thanks. Hey, wait a sec, you know who John Belushi is?"

"Yeah, I know who he is," I said. I watched "Saturday Night Live" every week.

"You wanna meet him? He came down for a few hours to hang out."

"Where is he?" I asked. The Benny walked to the office door and pointed through the glass pane. In the distance, I could see frantic splashing in the swimming pool.

"There, the guy in yellow trunks." A blur of yellow sprung off the diving board into a mass of limbs and glittery reflections of sunlight. "That's him! Come on, I'll introduce ya."

John Belushi swimming at my hotel pool. Cheebugger, Cheebugger, Cheebugger! No Coke – Pepsi! And the Samurai!

Now if it were any other non-guest swimming in my pool, I would have told him to leave. Our insurance didn't cover them. And anyway, the beach was just a mile away. Who wanted to swim in a pool when the ocean was so close?

Jesus, John Belushi. That guy probably got laid every night. And every morning.

"Hey, I gotta get back to the pool," said the Benny. "Come down and I'll introduce ya." He stepped out of the office. I really wanted to go, but my mother, who was fast asleep in the bedroom, would demand to know why I'd abandoned my post – something I'd never done before.

Still, I just had to go. I'd risk a screaming session with my mother to meet John Belushi. I'd never met a celebrity before.

I came up with a plan. I could tell my mother that I had had to go refill the soda machines because a customer had come down to the office and complained that they were empty. After all, the customer was always right.

I took a thick ring of keys hanging below the Marlboro clock, stuck a "BACK IN 15 MINUTES" sign in the office window, and locked the door behind me. I liked that sign because the customers never knew when those 15 minutes had started.

I unlocked the supply closet next door to Room 3 and dragged out crates of canned soda.

The Fiorellos were sitting in plastic lawn chairs in the shade of the edge of the roof. In the winter, they'd come into the office and sit and blah blah blah for hours with my mother or just themselves, but in the summer, they pulled out folding chairs and sat by their car. After going through the effort of changing into swimming attire, they couldn't be bothered to walk down to the pool. The *National Enquirer* was draped across Mrs. Fiorello's lap. It looked like a wind-strewn newspaper along the freckled fat of the land. Peter Fiorello stared up into the sky, his sunglasses reflecting fuzzy white clouds. Two fingers were wedged into his waistband.

"Peter, look at the young man working so hard in the summer!" said Mrs. Fiorello. "Maybe you should get a summer job, too." She patted the hairy lump that oozed over the rim of Peter Fiorello's shorts.

"My job all year round is to be a fat slob next to you and make you look good," he said. His eyebrows jerked above the rim of his sunglasses and a splotch of blue tattoo ink on his chest quivered. "I make her look real good, don't I? Just like Suzanne Sommers."

Mrs. Fiorello was as far from Suzanne Sommers as men were from women. God, I couldn't even imagine sitting in the car with Mrs. Fiorello, much less being in bed with her. Then again, Peter Fiorello wasn't going to star in any eight-millimeter films this year.

I threw on a case of 7-Up, The UnCola, onto the handtruck, followed by a case of Tab diet cola and two cases of local sodas – Briardale Cola and Howdy! orange soda. They were cheaper than Coca-Cola and Sunkist, and tasted like it. Mrs. Fiorello opened her hands and shook her palms at the case of Tab.

"Oh, that's what I need! The One-Calorie Soda! I can't find it anywhere."

"She doesn't even know it causes cancer."

"Well, even if it causes cancer, Peter, it can't be as bad as your cigars, you know."

"But I look good holding a cigar up. Gives me an excuse not to talk because my mouth is full. Showing people you drink Tab tells them, 'I'm fat! I need help!

Get me on a diet!' She looks great anyway. Doesn't need to lose anything but her mother."

"Peter, that's terrible! I love my mother. You love my mother, too!"

"I have to fill the soda machine," I said, anxious to be on my way. They both waved as I shoved off with the handtruck. The three soda machines, which were next to the pool's shallow end, stood against the walls of a defunct hamburger stand that had closed years before we'd bought the hotel. The glass sliding doors to the stand were still intact, no cracks or chips. If you cupped your hands to the glass, you could see dusty sheets thrown over rectangular kitchen equipment in the darkness inside.

My eyes swept the pool area, lingering over asses and tits, but I didn't see the Benny who took the bottle opener, or Belushi's yellow trunks. I looked a little longer, then decided to fill the soda machines while I waited.

The soda key was special. Instead of being flat, it consisted of a small crown of metal that plugged into a circular slot on each machine. One machine held just Briardale Cola, the other held 7-Up and Howdy! orange soda, and the third held Briardale Cola and Tab. Each machine held about 200 cans of soda that went for 35 cents a pop. They would run out after only a few days in the summertime, and I had to refill them right before and again during the busy weekends. The cigarette machine, which charged 75 cents for a pack and a book of matches with blank covers, would run out, too, but the cigarette guy filled that one up, not me.

Filling the machines meant pain. I would get two deep red grooves on each hand between the thumb and the index finger from unloading all the six-packs. When I complained, my mother would slap at my hands.

"That's nothing!" she'd say, "You're not bleeding. You're still young. When you're old, then you can complain about your body." The next day, I'd have bruise marks where the red had been, with a bunch of tiny blue and red dots in the grooves of the calluses like specks of glitter caught under my skin. I would show my mother, but she would just laugh, saying they would disappear after a few days. And they did.

Tab was always the last drink to sell out. Even the Bennys would rather drink Briardale Cola with its horse-head logo or Howdy! with its stupid buck-toothed clown mascot instead of Tab. Belushi would never drink Tab.

Out of curiosity, I tried one. It tasted like liquefied dead bugs coated in pesticide and mashed into my mouth. I turned the can on its side and the soda foamed as it hit the dirt. I locked up the machines and took a closer look at the swimmers, walking around the perimeter of the pool. John Belushi was nowhere to be seen. Some guys fit his dimensions, but no one was wearing yellow trunks. Bottle Opener Benny was also gone.

CHAPTER 6

The permanent population of our town could never sustain the businesses and "public works" of the area. I read an editorial about it in the paper. Everybody hated the Bennys, but we needed them to come in and buy our food and beer, buy parking spaces, pay for beach tags to pin on their swimsuits, and rent our rooms. After one stormy summer, the township raised property taxes for the year, citing the drop in tourism. After that, the extra drunk-driving, vandalism, and litter in the summers didn't seem so bad.

The teachers needed the Bennys, too. When school was out, you could spot your teachers working summer jobs, most of them no more glamorous than what teenagers would do. They wouldn't be perched by the fryer in McDonald's, but they might end up like Miss Creach as a cashier at Food World. Watching her bag up groceries and make change for smelly guys in shorts with hairy legs and bare feet, I lost respect for Miss Creach, even though she was the one who'd taught me about how plankton fit in the food chain. When she worked at Food World, she wore an apron that read,

"I'm here to help you!" across the front pocket. She looked like a high-school dropout.

"Hi, Miss Creach," I said.

"Hello there," she said as a minor logjam of Slim Jims and Fruit Roll-Ups advanced on the conveyor belt along with bread, a box of rice, eggs, ground beef, peppers, onions, and apples. Slim Jims and Fruit Roll-Ups covered two of the four food groups – red meat and fruit. Miss Creach frowned, like she caught me with crib notes. "Your mother know what you eat?"

"No. She has no idea."

"You sure you don't want two bags?" she asked as I stuffed everything into a brown paper bag.

"I got my bike, so I can only take one," I said.

"Drink some milk, okay? Or else your bones are going to stop growing," she replied, wiping her arm against her forehead.

I got onto my bike, one hand on the handlebar and one holding the bag. The bike had come with a basket in front, but I'd torn it off because baskets looked gay. I was fine with one hand.

My parents sat in the kitchen eating Chinese food, and I was in the living room, eating a bowl of Sloppy Joe and watching "M*A*S*H." Two Korean women were sitting on Klinger's cot, crying. In the background, I could hear my mother and father talking in Chinese. Actually, my mother was talking in Chinese and my father was saying, "Umgh, umgh," as he ate.

"You want to open burger stand?" asked my mother.

She was speaking in English, so it was understood that I was being addressed.

"What?"

"Turn down TV!" she ordered. Canned laughter washed over the sound of the Korean women sobbing.

"I can hear you fine! Why do you want to open it?" I looked over at my parents. They were fixed in a brightly lit realm of tile, wood, and table, while I was sitting cross legged on the worn rug of the living room. They were in a completely different world.

"Come over here! You can't hear me! You should eat with us!"

"I don't like the way your food smells! Just tell me what you want!" I said, getting annoyed.

"We want you run burger stand on weekend. People get hungry and go across street to Barnhouse. You know how – you cook hamburgers. You cook Sloppy Joe." The Barnhouse was a drive-in across the highway from the hotel. Bennys would pick up burgers, fries, and onion rings there, and come back and sit by the pool. I was always sweeping up soggy, flattened cartons smeared with oil, ketchup, and ants.

The burger stand by the pool had been closed for years, but the equipment was still there, alongside the crates of hotel supplies we stored in the space. The only times I'd go inside was to get spare light bulbs or ashtrays.

The scene inside the hamburger stand reminded me of those *National Geographic* features where they'd run a waterproof camera through the former living quarters of undersea shipwrecks. It was dark and murky and filled with drifting particles. Layers of gunk coated all the flat surfaces. Chairs were strewn about as if they had been abandoned in haste. And surrounding everything was an eerie stillness. Fixing that place up would be way harder than flipping burgers.

"I can't run that place by myself. I need some help!" I yelled.

"From one to five, you're going be open. Saturday and Sunday. All you do is play Atari, anyway." There wasn't much sense in arguing that point. When all the rooms were rented, there wasn't anything to do in the afternoons but sit in the office and tell people we didn't have any more rooms or make change for the phone or for the candy or cigarette machine. But I still had to sit there.

I was trapped at the hotel, watching people older than me having fun. Fun that was supposed to be mine. I was the kid. Instead, I was just another employee at the hotel. I wanted to be a customer and get that air conditioning, get those girls, get some fun.

That hotel owned us. Reopening the burger stand just meant adding another room and more chores to our prison.

A local woman named Nancy helped with the cleaning on Sundays in the summer when the Bennys checked out and nearly all of the hotel's rooms had to be straightened up. Nancy would start working at around 11 a.m., which was check-out time, and finish around seven. For lunch, she'd sit on the bed in one of the dirty rooms, eat a Snickers bar, and watch the second half of a half-hour sitcom.

Nancy wore rubber gloves when she picked up used condoms and joints. She disposed of the pornography more discretely than my mom, but I fished it back out of the garbage at night when she was gone. Her long hair was the color of paint on a broken-down barn, and it shook from side to side as she scrubbed or vacuumed. Nancy worked hard for the $30 we paid her for the day, and she also got tips. She was only 40, but her face was badly wrinkled. Her husband walking out on her had left permanent marks.

Nancy talked incessantly, but she only had three themes – loneliness, love, and her daughter Anne-Marie.

"Ah, Jim and I got married too young, you know? You try and fight so hard to be an adult, and when you get there, everybody's trying to claw their way back. But an older man can always get a younger woman and get halfway back, so you're lucky you're a boy, kid. Just like Jim. Ah, if you're a girl, you've only got the television, and you keep it on because when you turn it off, you see your reflection in the black screen."

"Ah, these kids, all the drinking and sex, I like to see kids having fun. I think it's okay, stay young, hold on to your dreams. Don't let other people tell you what to do. Ah, you're too young to know love. This room, this is what young love smells like."

"Ah, I always tell Anne-Marie it's okay to be confused. Sometimes the only way to find yourself is when you're confused. You've got to turn off all the voices in your head one by one until you find that last one that's your own. You have to experience everything before you can make decisions. Experience is more important than education, Einstein said that. See, you thought I was stupid. The secretaries from the principal's office keep calling me about Anne-Marie and ask me why I can't control her. I tell them, 'Hey, look how far high school got you!' Ah, you've got to climb every mountain."

One day, when I was helping Nancy wring out a pile of beer-soaked sheets in the driveway, she said Anne-Marie was going to work at the burger stand with me.

Anne-Marie was her right name, but my mother always called her "Annie-Marie." She was 16 and was going to drop out of high school as soon as it was legally possible. Until then, she was cutting altogether. I'd only seen her a few times when she'd come to drop off and pick up Nancy on Sundays, but seeing the silhouette of her upper torso behind the tinted glass of her car made my skin feel hot and prickly, even when I was standing in the shade.

I would stare at the little charms on the bracelet Anne-Marie wore on her left ankle when she stepped from the car. She would lean over on the open door and flip her shades up into her dark red hair. The door and tinted glass would block out most of her body, except for a space from the wound-down window that framed her belly button in a rectangle.

She wasn't prettier than Lee Anderson, but she was sexier because she knew how to move her tits and ass. There was no way she was a virgin.

I was thinking hard about her while I was scrubbing

away at the crusted grill. I'm not sure when the burger stand was last open, but they hadn't cleaned up before closing. Someone had left behind a portable stereo. The radio didn't work, but there was a tape in it, *The Byrds' Greatest Hits*. After hearing "Mr. Tambourine Man" for the fourth time, I took out the tape and destroyed it with a milk crate.

A discolored sheet of paper taped by the light switch gave directions on how to clean the grill. Who knew there were so many steps to cleaning a grill? I rubbed the grill with Brillo pads and a porous brick that smelled like a bad fart as it wore down. I scraped all the solids off the grill with a spatula. Then I paper-toweled a layer of oil over the cleaned surface.

I dragged all the hotel supplies into a corner and threw a sheet over them, so no one would notice. The four flimsy tables seemed to be made from artificial Christmas tree bases and were so scummy, I didn't want to go over them with a sponge. That would have taken hours. Instead, I pulled them outside and sprayed them down with the pool hose. It took a whole week to get that place ready, and the heavy cleanser fumes killed a lot of my common sense.

By the time we opened, most of the kitchen was still pretty raunchy, but everything the customers could see looked clean. After I wiped down the fluorescent lights, the counter shone like a shelf in K-Mart after the blue-light special sold out.

The menu, spelled out in white plastic letters on a

Pepsi sign board, read: "BURGER $1.50 CHEESE-BURGER $1.75 FRIES $1.25." There was only one 5, so the other two were S's. Everything was 25 cents cheaper than the Barnhouse. We didn't sell any drinks, because the soda machines were right outside.

A rack of snack chips sat by the cash machine. Each dinky bag of Fritos, Ruffles, Lays, and Doritos was marked "NOT FOR INDIVIDUAL SALE," but I went over them with a thick black laundry marker. I had bought three six-pack Snax Pax for 99 cents each and now each bag was priced at 60 cents.

With only three things on the menu – really only two, – it would be pretty hard to fuck things up, even for a wannabe high-school dropout and a 12-year-old boy. My parents had checked to see if there was a minimum age for working a grill or deep fryer. There wasn't any if an adult was present. My father was officially down as the supervisor on duty, but how he was supervising from his workshop almost a quarter of a mile away was beyond me. If the burger stand went up in a mushroom cloud, would he run to get there before the cops and pretend he'd been there the entire time?

That first day, I was wondering how we would get away with charging 25 cents for a slice of cheese when Anne-Marie walked in. She was wearing shorts and a white tanktop. I thought all her curves were a little soft, but in the right places.

Because there were no customers to serve, I constantly found Anne-Marie bending over the counter, leaning on the rack of the grill, or slouching over a few boxes. She'd brush her hair behind her ears and turn to face me, smiling – a basic pose from the porn magazines. My body couldn't help but respond.

"Oh, Jesus, what's this?" she asked, rubbing my cock under my corduroy shorts. "How old are you?" Her hand hadn't left my lump.

"I'm 12," I gulped. We'd been working less than an hour together. It was all unfolding like a letter to *Hustler*, where women always made the first move. I put my hands on her ass.

"I'm impressed," Anne-Marie said, letting her fingers slide off and slipping her body out of my grip. I took a deep breath and felt my head throb. Then I swallowed the wrong way and coughed.

The place was still empty. Two people had stopped in earlier, but they'd only wanted change for the soda machines. At around 2:30, I fried up two cheeseburgers and fries for us. I took some change out of the register and bought two Briardale colas. I watched Anne-Marie make zig zags in the ketchup splotch with her fries.

"Let's fuck," I said, feeling Vincent's voice coming out of my well-greased mouth. She laughed and I felt a light spray of chewed food on my hands.

"What did you say? You're a dirty kid, you know that? I can't believe you said that." Anne-Marie shook her head, but she was smiling.

"I want to get laid this summer," I explained.

"I gotta boyfriend so I can't fuck, but I can give you a hand job."

"Can't you at least blow me?"

"No, I don't wanna cheat, you know?"

"Can you give me a hand job now?"

"Wait until I finish my soda. Let me wash my hands, too. We hafta make sure nobody comes in."

"Should I wash also?"

"No, you don't have to. I just want to clean my hands right now. They feel gross." She sipped the last of her soda from her straw, and I could hear the can bottoming out.

We went behind the counter, and I put my elbows up against the wood shelf next to the grill. Her hands quickly unzipped my shorts. She was holding a wad of dry napkins in her right hand as her left hand pumped away.

"You're going to make the girls really happy," she said, pulling and twisting. I came in about 10 seconds. She wiped me off with the napkin and threw it away.

"Can I see your tits?" I asked. The pool area was full, but no one was coming into the reopened snack bar. Anne-Marie smiled.

"No, you can't, I have a boyfriend. Well, you can feel them." I put my hands up against her breasts. They were a lot softer than I thought they'd be. I squeezed and saw her nipples straining against the tight fabric. I pressed her left nipple.

Anne-Marie moved in her arm and brought my hands down with a sweep of her elbow. "That's enough now."

My eyes moved down her front to the zipper of her shorts. There were a few loose threads fringed around her thighs.

"I know what you're thinking," said Anne-Marie. "And the answer is 'No.'"

All we ended up making that day was $2.50 when some Benny bought two orders of fries.

That night, I was so excited about my first hand job, I jerked off two more times. Let Vincent call me a fag now.

The health inspector dropped by the stand in the middle of the week, before we could open for the next weekend. He looked like a giant walrus with his puffy cheeks, mustache, and beard.

I wrestled the lock open and flipped all the light switches on.

"Where's the supervisor?" he asked.

"Down in the crawlspace," I said. The inspector wrote this down.

In the routine checkup that followed, he found seven "severe" violations. He was mad that there was no soap at the sink where we were supposed to be washing our hands. He stopped checking after seven, because four alone would shut a place down. I saw the phrase "walls greasy to the touch" on his report pad.

"When are you people going to learn…" he muttered as he left the hamburger stand.

"You're so fucking gay!" I yelled after him as he walked stiffly to his van. He came back with a sign and taped it to the door.

"Now lock this place up and don't touch that sign, you little son of a bitch!"

I went into the basement and found my father, who was fixing a stack of metal bed frames fresh from the demolition company. Some of them had metal coasters, some had swivel wheels, and some used to have swivel wheels.

"The health inspector came and shut down the hamburger stand," I told him.

"Did he take keys?"

"No, but he put up a big notice saying that we're closed by order of the Department of Health and Safety."

"Open burger stand not a good idea," he said. "Not my idea." He would never say more than about four words in the presence of my mother, but when we were working alone, we would sometimes talk.

"Now we have to eat all the leftover hamburger buns."

"Bring back to store and get money back."

"It's only about $10."

"You think $10 is nothing? These bed frames are $10!" I went back upstairs to the kitchen and got the receipt. But I decided to wait before going back. I was too embarrassed to return the food in front of Miss Creach.

The following day, my mother called Nancy and told her the stand was shut down for good and that Anne-Marie didn't have to come back. Listening to that phone call broke my heart.

CHAPTER 7

As the summer drew to a close, the days grew shorter and more humid. The Bennys put on a brave face, sweating out their last shot at getting a tan.

The dying sunlight lingered just above the horizon, stretching the shadows of the coniferous trees surrounding the hotel longer and longer until they were shady, swaying fingers waving good-bye to the Bennys. Business thinning out in the middle of the week meant that the hotel only reached full capacity on the weekends. It also meant fewer women. My already slim chance of getting laid at the hotel was shrinking even more.

I sat behind the hotel desk, staring out across the lawn that sat in the middle of the U. As it grew darker, the grass I had neglected to cut for the past few weeks dimmed into a shiny black. A light breeze sent it streaming in waves. The lawn looked like the surface of a deep, murky sea full of secrets.

Dinner smells and sounds of eating drifted in from the kitchen, but I was full since I'd already eaten three slices of pepperoni pizza from one of the rooms. We never ordered out because it was too expensive, so finding pizza in a room was almost as good as finding hard-core porn with a blonde in it. The pizza box had been open, lying on the bed like another suitcase to pack. I checked for cigarette ashes or butts in the box before taking a bite. The slices were cold, colder than room temperature. Oil from under the scab of cheese dripped down onto my socks. After three stiff slices, I felt a sharp, greasy pain in the right side of my stomach that moved slowly downward.

I was mentally preparing myself for another night in the crawlspace with my father, who was eating a small herd in hamburger meat. He ate a lot of meat because he said it helped him work hard.

With fewer people at the hotel, the end of the summer was the best time to get renovations done. And there was a hell of a lot of work to do. When it was busy, bathroom fixtures and parts of the floor stayed broken for practically the entire summer simply because the rooms were never vacant long enough to fix up. Angry or drunk men liked to punch holes in closet doors or kick in the sheetrock walls. These were pretty easy to fix with a little putty mix, but we wouldn't repaint the patches until September. Then I would go around with a pail and a dropcloth, getting all of them in one shot. In the meantime, some rooms looked like they had been draped in giraffe skin because there were so many patches.

I yawned and cringed at the pain in my stomach. I hoped the pizza had been okay to eat. I made a fist with my left hand and punched the spot hard twice. I'd learned that trick from Vincent. He used to run track in high school, and whenever he cramped up, he would just beat it out.

"It's a psychological thing," he said. "When the pain from the punches goes away, it don't hurt as much. If it still hurts a lot, it means you have to punch harder."

When I heard the dreaded sound of the sink and clanking dishes, I knew dinner was over and it was time to work again. I'd be glad when school started again because then I'd have a good excuse not to work late every night. I went to get the flashlight, the lantern, and two pairs of work gloves.

My father and I were under Room 37. The wood in the bathroom floor had rotted away. We could see the tell-tale concentric rings of discoloration in the panels above us. I was squatting in the dirt, holding the lantern up. The orange electric cord snaked off into the darkness. The crawlspace was long and wide, but only about four feet high. If you crouch-walked too fast through it, you'd knock your head against a faucet or a bend in the pipes that ran across the top of the crawlspace. I had to hold the lantern up at an angle, otherwise the vertical slats of wood would cast shadows on the work area.

My father tore at the rotted wood with the claw end of a hammer. His face, which was illuminated from below, looked meaty and sweaty. I could smell charred beef as he breathed through his mouth in time to the hammer swinging. Sometimes he had to put the hammer down to rest.

Pieces of wood flicked onto my face like insects onto a

light bulb at night, and damp flakes went down the front of my shirt. I nearly lost my balance when a fat splinter fell against my eyelid. The lantern swung crazily and landed on its side.

"It's just wood," said my father, handing the lantern back to me. "Don't worry about it. Just pieces of wood. Who cares?"

"But it's rotten. It might make me sick."

"Don't be a fool," he said, as his lips and eyebrows, exaggerated by the lighting, shifted between incredulity and annoyance. "Wood never make anybody sick."

"I won't be able to do this when school starts in two weeks."

"Then you got a lot of work to do in next two weeks. You have to finish putty holes in even-number rooms. You have to measure the windows in Number 23 and Number 25 and get glass from hardware store. There some other things I wrote down you have to do, too."

"I know, I have the list in my bedroom. You taped it to my closet door."

"Next year I show you how to use blowtorch and soldering so you can make copper tubing we need for sinks. Very easy."

"All this stuff you're showing me you don't even need to go to college for. Doing this makes me forget everything I learn in school. Doing this makes me stupid. I don't want to work here the rest of my life."

"You have to have some practical knowledge. You don't want to learn Chinese, you don't want to eat Chinese food, so you can learn how to fix floors. I only wish I learned something about car repair so I don't get cheated."

My father hated being cheated, and always felt that everyone was out to trick him. He had taken his transistor radio apart and put it back together again so he could figure out how to fix electronics and not be fooled by technicians who charged more for labor than parts. Then they started using those modified screws that you needed a special screwdriver for. That was when my father stopped buying electronics. Our stereo consisted of an old radio and a turntable built into a bulky wooden cabinet upstairs. We only had two records – the soundtrack of the original cast of "Oklahoma!" and Johnny Cash's "I Walk The Line." Johnny Cash was the first music I'd ever heard.

I reached with my free hand for a clean new plank of wood and handed it to my father. Rotted wood, looking like strips of beef jerky, lay strewn around us on the floor, along with bent nails, pieces of cut-off pipe, and crushed beer cans from repairmen the previous owners had used. No one else was crazy enough to try to fix the place themselves.

"See here," said my father, tapping a plastic pipe over his head. "Repairman used plastic, not copper. Try to cheat." It made him happy that no plumbers, electricians, or construction crews would be down here in the crawlspace while we owned the place.

Two more new planks and the floor was fixed. We fixed five more floors before he let me go to sleep.

Labor Day weekend was the traditional last hurrah for the Bennys. I saw Vincent as he was stuffing t-shirts into his car trunk. Patty, who had endured another summer and was still his girlfriend, was sitting up front on the passenger side.

"Tough luck, no score for you this summer," said Vincent. His eyes were red, and he was moving slow.

"I got a girl to jerk me off," I said.

"Yeah, that's a start. Something to build on. Just find some chick in school this year. They're curious when they're young."

"I got someone in mind."

"Who's this?" he asked, wrapping an arm around my neck and walking me backwards. "Some unfuckable ugly-ass bitch?" Vincent was play-choking me, and his beer breath was knocking me out. He switched arms and shoved my nose into his sweaty, smelly armpit. Patty leaned on the horn. He loosened up on me.

"This girl, she's beautiful." I stammered. The horn sounded a second time. Patty screamed something but the windows were up and she sounded like she was under water.

"This shit again," muttered Vincent, releasing me completely. "I tell ya, I come back next summer, that cherry on your cock better be gone. I'm not fuckin' around, you know!"

He dipped into a foam cooler and fished out an open can of beer.

"Hey, you finish this," he shouted at me, shoving the can into my gut. It was about half-empty. "Drink it!

Don't look at me like that. Fucking drink it, pussy!"

I choked down my first beer. It tasted like foamy metal.

"Thought I was going to have to lock you in the trunk to get you to drink up," Vincent muttered as he stepped into the car.

CHAPTER 8

When the last day of the Labor Day weekend hit, the summer season was over. The town looked like a tornado warning was in effect and a massive evacuation was underway. Bennys piled into their cars and pointed them North for the fall, winter, and spring. Cars with New Jersey and New York license plates were lined up, smashed headlight to dented trunk. That was when the town released all its anger against the Bennys. Locals would line up along the highway that led back to the city with signs reading, "GO HOME, BENNYS!" and "GET THE HELL OUT!"

I walked along the highway to the hardware store to get the type of AC adapter that screws into a light-bulb socket. My bike tire was out of commission, and I didn't feel like fixing it now. There was too much broken glass on the road, and I was repairing so many flats, I felt like I was running a bike shop.

A local man, wearing a Pac-Man Fever baseball cap, a tank top, and a tank-like belly, shouted across the bottled-up highway at me.

"Hey, you fucking chink, you get the hell out of my town!"

I stopped and stared at him. He smiled at me a little, then waved and turned back to the Bennys.

My new teacher in the fall was Mr. Hendrickson. In the summer, he worked as a rent-a-cop pounding the boardwalk. Mr. Hendrickson showed authority as he weaved through pedestrian traffic, his huge frame sweeping through the boisterous crowds by the boardwalk games. I'd see him moving through people like a shark fin above water when I stopped at the boardwalk for a game of Berserk! or Space Invaders before going to the hardware store.

But he also had to sweep up broken bottles, popsicle sticks, and other trash. That wasn't too different from what I had to do. When he was young, he probably would have fit right in with the Bennys. Now, his six-foot-six frame looked more bloated than brute. But there was no doubt that the man could do some damage, even in his overweight and graying state.

About a week before school was going to start, as the Bennys were having their last shot at destroying our town, a mini-brawl had broken out on Mr. Hendrickson's turf. Three shirtless, drunk guys were grappling with each other, knocking over folding chairs by the lemon-ade slush and cheesefries stand. Mr. Hendrickson stepped in and grabbed a Benny with each hand, but that left the third guy free. Mr. Hendrickson woke up flat on his back with two other rent-a-cops standing over him and a gash on his face that required stitches.

I'd read about the incident in the paper. They'd put

the story on the same page as the television listings. The name "Hendrickson" stood out because I knew he was going to be my teacher that fall. I saw the scar the first day of school. I thought a broken bottle would leave a circular mark, but instead there was a thin, crusty scab about two inches long that ran from the center of his forehead to the top of the bridge of his nose. The skin around it was puffy like a caterpillar.

Mr. Hendrickson had a big St. Bernard's head, jiggling jowls, and eyes that dripped behind glasses smudged with greasy fingerprints. He reeked of alcohol and cigarette smoke, like one of our hotel rooms, only we tried to cover the smell up with air fresheners. For some reason, he thought that nobody could hear what he said when he took his glasses off.

"Now this is Greece and this is Italy," Mr. Hendrickson said, circling all of Europe and the northern part of Africa with the skittering tip of his wooden pointer. "The Romans and the Greeks had philosophy and art. Sometimes they had to fight, too. They were some of the world's most advanced civilizations ever. The United States has been around for only two centuries. We probably won't last as long as the Romans and the Greeks. We'll probably be conquered by Japan or maybe even Mexico someday."

Then his glasses came off, and he rubbed each lens with his tie, muttering, "Goddamn, fucking bullshit. Tired of this shit."

The glasses popped back onto his face, as simple as on a Mr. Potatohead, and the lecture continued.

"Mexico was the last country to invade the United States, not England, in the War of 1812. A lot of people don't know that. It was Pancho Villa. And a lot of people talk about the bombing of Pearl Harbor. Hawaii wasn't even a state yet! The next time the japs bomb the U.S., it'll be San Francisco or Seattle. Definitely something on the West Coast."

The first week, all the kids were terrified by Mr. Hendrickson's Dr. Jekyll/Mr. Hyde routine. But we soon realized he was harmless, and got used to it.

I ignored the lectures because I read the right stuff in the textbook. The only thing that changed through the year with Mr. Hendrickson was that his scar healed into what looked like the fake stitches on a Nerf football.

School was well underway, but summer wasn't truly over until it was time to drain the pool. I sat in a battered pool chair next to Peter and Mrs. Fiorello, watching the noisy pump chug out water and flood the lawn.

"What are you studying in school?" asked Mrs. Fiorello.

"Greece." It was only the second week, so I was really only fitting on book covers cut from shopping bags.

"Yeah, the Greeks were the first civilized people in this world," said Peter. "The buildings they put up back then are still standing now."

"How old are they?" asked Mrs. Fiorello.

"Millions of years, from when dinosaurs were still around."

"The dinosaurs died out before there were people," I corrected. Peter threw his hands up in the air. A small clump of ash from his cigar skittered across his bare chest.

"Who's to say, no one really knows," said Peter. "It was way before I was born and way before you were born. They'll be here long after we're dead." Steady splish-splashes from the pump continued to sound in the background.

"You know what happens when you die?" asked Mrs. Fiorello, adding in a hushed voice: "I don't want to scare you, but I've told your mother that you should go to church."

I had thought about going to church. Probably a lot of girls there. Maybe the ones in church had tits. I wasn't going to find out, though. I was too busy cleaning rooms Sundays.

My parents never read the Bible, although every room had a copy. Why go to church? Jesus wouldn't bring in more johns.

The newly installed chain-link fence closed off the hotel's back yard, which would have been a shortcut to the church. We had to put up the fence because our neighbors to the back complained of finding Bennys in their pools or beer bottles and cans on their lawn.

The pump chugged away, and the level of the pool sank a fraction of an inch. A thin film of green stretched across the surface like a slice of cheese on day-old pizza. The Fiorellos got up and left, Mrs. Fiorello yawning and Peter scratching his forehead with the end of the cigar that had been in his mouth. I took a look at the pool furniture around me, dreading the task that awaited me. I would have to drag them all one by one and stack them up in the once-again dead burger stand. When I was done with that, it would be time to pull out the splinters that bit through the leather work gloves.

I closed my eyes and listened to the chugging sound of the pump. It sounded like a worn-out heart.

CHAPTER 9

In the late fall and winter months, when business was dead and even johns barely trickled in, we dropped the rates to $60 a week. The loneliest guys you'd ever seen would straggle in. These old white men might have crawled out from under railroad platforms. They didn't get much sun and their clothes were damp and dirty. They were mostly widowers abandoned by their own children, of whom they still spoke fondly. They lived off of Social Security checks and Twinkies and Suzy-Qs. God knows they didn't have enough money to get drunk.

They would come into the office and talk away like it was a general store and we were sitting down to a checkers game on the flat end of an upright barrel. My mother hated talking to these old men, and when I came home from school, she'd make a quick exit and force me to keep them company, or at least to make sure they didn't walk off with a newspaper without paying for it.

Around March, the weekly rate would go back up to $125, squeezing their cash flow, and the old timers would leave. Sometimes they'd come back the next winter. Sometimes you heard that they'd died.

The stragglers came back again around Halloween. How appropriate. These lonely old guys never earned more than minimum wage their entire lives and had more fingers than teeth. Like a flock that instinctively knew where to fly to find warmth, they honed in on and migrated to residences on the shore, where rents were dirt cheap in the off-season. All the young people were gone, which probably suited the old men fine. When the hookers and johns rolled in and out, they were already dead asleep.

The temperature drop chilled the seasonal businesses of the shore. The boardwalk stands stripped of their toy prizes looked like a row of abandoned outhouses. The drive-in across the street pulled its wooden benches up over the glass windows, chaining them with their legs sticking out, as if preparing against an amphibious landing. The hardware store cut back on their hours and was only open on the weekends. Sometimes hotel repairs would have to wait a week or more before I could buy the necessary part.

The hotel shut down most of the rooms, leaving only around 20 open. That was about the right number: we could still expect about three or four johns at any one time, four or five people were actual customers who would spend the night, and we needed about eight rooms for the old men.

For $60 a week, the old men would get an electric hot plate with two burners and a tiny refrigerator that could hold about two boxes of Twinkies. They also got a portable electric heater. Those rooms got pretty damn cold – the drafts through the battered air conditioners bolted into the wall neutralized the power of the central heat.

There were never enough heaters to go around, so when someone complained about the cold, my parents would give mine out, then theirs. Sometimes I went to sleep to the buzzing warmth of the heater only to wake up cold in the middle of the night, the glowing metal strips replaced by darkness, my heater given away to a customer.

At the hotel I learned the life cycle of white men. Go to school, get a job, get drunk and laid every weekend, get married, have kids, get old, watch your family abandon you, and live off of Social Security until you die.

Every day I saw the various stages. Kids in school. A john stopping by at three in the morning. An old man waiting for the water on the hotplate to boil for instant coffee, saying he'd have the rent first thing next week. Peter Fiorello was the only old white man I saw who still had a wife and seemed to be happy.

White women were a little different. After they finished high school, they worked at fast-food joints or, if they looked good enough, landed in the porn magazines. If they were really unlucky, they might end up turning tricks in our rooms. There was no place for old white women at the shore. The only old white women I saw besides Mrs. Fiorello were on television.

Something strange about those Fiorellos.

When they stopped by on weekends in the winter, the Fiorellos spent nearly the whole day in the office, talking with my mother. Through the closed door to the office, I

freckles probably covered her fat-swollen tits and ass cheeks. Sweat was slick on her forehead and probably between her thighs, too. Her pussy probably smelled worse than licking-tuna-can jokes implied.

"You're such a cute Chinese boy, you should speak some more and be proud of what you are," Mrs. Fiorello said. "Really, it's okay."

I cleared my throat, opened the door to the living room, and withdrew to the kitchen. The biscuits were hardening. After I finished choking them down, I squeezed some detergent onto a sponge and wiped down the baking tray, the butter knife, and my plate. I took the dishrag and wiped the vinyl place setting until it glistened.

Then I looked at the list of things I had to do, which was written in all capitals on a yellow, lined sheet torn from a legal-sized notepad. A magnet from East Coast Distributors held the paper to the fridge. The instructions read like telegrams, with their clipped English and lack of punctuation.

"ONE: IF THERE IS ICE ON POOL COVER SHEET BREAK IT UP AND THREW IT AWAY OVER FENCE ONTO GRASS NOT DRIVEWAY

"TWO: SHAKE SALT ON SIDEWALK FROM ROOM 12 AND FROM ROOM 11A

"THREE: GO TO HARDWARE STORE AND BUY THREE LIGHT SOCKET AC ADAPTERS GET MONEY FROM MOMMY.

"FOUR: PICK UP ALL LOOSE TRASH ON DRIVEWAY CIGARET CAN BOTTLE."

Reading the list, I always had to insert "the" in the

right places. It was already an automatic process from years of listening to my parents talk.

Nothing too strenuous today. There was no ice on the pool covering, and sprinkling salt was child's play.

The worst had been when my father bought surplus railroad ties and concrete bunkers to keep the Bennys from driving over the lawn. New Jersey Transit dropped them off, but refused to hammer in the iron spokes needed to keep them in place. That became my job. The calluses I had from slamming that sledgehammer down hundreds of times that weekend will be with me until I wrap my hands around a walking stick.

I went outside and threw salt around. I moved like an old man wandering around a park, feeding pigeons. I thought about what it would be like to be one of the old men. Old and worn out from years of getting laid hundreds of times, living by myself, eating Chocodiles and fruit pies.

As I drew closer to the Fiorellos' room, the announcements from a football game grew louder. I stood outside the door, one hand on the plastic scoop, the other holding the bucket of granulated salt. Mrs. Fiorello was still in the office, gabbing away. She had waved with manic intensity through the office window as I passed, but I'd given only a polite nod in response.

Through the curved triangle of space between the closed curtains, I saw Peter Fiorello watching the football game. It was half-time, and the cheerleaders were building pyramids. His back was turned to me and I saw his cigar wiggle.

Was this the end of the life cycle of all white men? Watching football in a hotel room? What happened to old Chinese men? Did they all withdraw into basement workshops like my father?

I had a hard time understanding Frank, one of the off-season old-timers, because he couldn't pronounce the letter "t." My mother had enough trouble with people who spoke correct English. Frank had about three different plaid shirts and he never washed them. There was no laundry room at the hotel, but you could smell the hotel-bar soap on the clothes of the other old men.

Creases in Frank's filthy jeans were deepest at the knees, and it looked like broken chopsticks in his pant legs were supporting the fabric. He couldn't hold his right leg still, so he would stand at the counter and lean over sideways on his left elbow. Frank's right knee shook back and forth like a frog's leg hooked to a battery.

My mother sat on the stool behind the counter, legs crossed and hands thrust into her pockets. She hated being trapped in the office with Frank, but she wouldn't leave him alone there. The last time she walked out on one of these old men, he'd pissed on the office floor, then fallen asleep on the couch.

When I came in the office after school, she would get up, say good-bye to Frank, and gesture for me to sit on the stool. Over a number of excruciating afternoons, he told me a lot about his life. I never told him shit about mine.

The first time Frank saw me, he said, "You're preddy!"

It had obviously been a long time since he'd seen someone as young and as Asian as me. The last time had been when he was wandering the streets of Seoul, looking for hookers.

The fragments of Frank's story fit together as well as random pieces of peanut brittle.

When he was really young, he collected soda bottles in the streets of Chicago, drinking what was left in them before returning them to drug stores for a penny each. He was nicknamed "Pepsi" by the other kids.

He served in Europe in World War II, where he was shot in the leg before he ever had a chance to fire his gun. He was sent home, but later took an Army office job in South Korea, where he would meet two "ladies" every night.

Frank got married when he came back to the U.S., and an old Army buddy set him up in a lower management job with an oil company in Texas. He sat around all day, sharpening pencils with a pocket knife and passing cigars around for his newborn son.

Then he had a heart attack.

The company paid for his hospital bill, but wouldn't hire him again. The heart attack had left his speech slurred, and he lost partial control of the right side of his body. Even though he could still do his job, they told him that having him there was making everyone else in the office feel lousy.

His wife went to work cleaning houses while Frank stayed at home and drank. She took the kid with her to work when she realized that Frank fed him too much and never changed the diapers.

Frank started drinking heavily. His wife had to drive farther and farther to find houses to clean. He drank more and more. He couldn't stop. He never felt hungry. One day, his wife never came back. He didn't know where she or his son were. He could pass them in the street now and he wouldn't know who they were.

The government wanted to move Frank into a facility, but he refused to go. He applied for disability instead, using the checks for drinks. Then they cut him off. Years later, the Army found him again and gave him a lump-sum payment for veterans' benefits.

Now here he was, 30 years after Korea, still giving money to Koreans for cheap rooms.

"I'm not Korean, I'm an American," I said. That set him off.

"You haven'd erned da righd do call yourself an American undil you fighd for diss coundry! None of you people ever did shid for America! You only come here do dake our money! And led me dell you, we have courdesy in diss coundry. Yes we do. You see dad couch over dere?" He pointed to the office couch. "I never sad down dere and you people never invided me do sid. You see an old man like me wid my leg like diss, and you don even invide me do sid down!" Frank's whole body shook as he yelled, and his voice was unnaturally strong for his frail body. Then he glared at me and wobbled out of the office.

Frank stopped talking to me after that. If he knew I was around, he would come into the office, put his rent money on the counter, ring the bell, and leave.

The next time I cleaned Frank's room, I opened the suitcase that he kept under his bed. Inside was a *Playboy* from the 1960s.

As I picked it up, small round clippings slipped from the pages and fluttered to the floor. Picking up the pieces of paper, I broke into a sweat. They were women's faces, clipped from advertisements and fashion magazines. He'd made that old *Playboy* issue last by placing new faces on top of the nude bodies. Some of the faces were those of young children, boys and girls.

CHAPTER 10

By November, Mr. Hendrickson got too lazy to go down the hall to grade our tests. The weekly quizzes were scored electronically. He handed out computerized forms and we'd bubble in our answers with number two pencils. We didn't even write anymore, we just filled in Chinese-eye ovals on those forms. I forgot how to write cursive letters that weren't in my name. The tests would then be fed into the computer in the teacher's lounge. They would come back out with green dashes next to incorrect numbers and the final score printed out in crude dot-matrix numbers that made 1's, 7's, and 9's all look alike. The forms would be handed back without a single written comment on them. No sexy, curvy one-liners like the "Excellent!s" that Miss Creach used to write.

"My best student in the class will be in charge of grading," Mr. Hendrickson said. He held up a card.

"Here is the best student!" he bellowed, then called my name. I'd gotten a 99 on the big social-studies test from a month ago. Crispy punched my arm.

"You asshole! I got a 60!" he said.

"No talking!" yelled Mr. Hendrickson, as he walked

between the rows of desks handing back test forms. He grunted as he bent over to read student's names from the tags on the front of their desks.

"You got what you deserved, stupid," I whispered to Crispy. I looked across the room at Lee Anderson.

"Uh, oops," Mr. Hendrickson said, holding another card up. "Actually, it's a tie for top student!" He called Lee Anderson. "One hundred percentile!" Then he handed her test back. She's beautiful, she's got tits, and she's smart, I thought.

Lee's friends giggled and patted her. She was surrounded by so many girls all the time, it was nearly impossible to talk to her just one-on-one. I hadn't been able to say more than Hello without thinking I sounded stupid.

Crispy raised his hand. "Mr. Hendrickson, it's not a tie. He got a 99 and Lee got a hundred."

Mr. Hendrickson whirled around and yelled, "Shut up, you!" Then he calmed down and said, "These two are now in charge of grading your tests. I'm delegating my duties here so I can work more efficiently." He looked at me and Lee. "As for the two of you, you can watch each other to make sure there's no cheating."

He gave me the key to the teacher's lounge and handed a stack of our last three weekly tests to Lee.

We walked out the door as the class made kissy sounds behind us. I saw Mr. Hendrickson take off his glasses, and I knew they were in for it.

The lounge consisted of a shelf with a sink next to a refrigerator with a sign on it that said, "Label your lunch or lose it." It stunk of cigarettes like some of our hotel rooms. It was empty now, since the teachers only hung out there at lunch time. Bright fluorescent lights gave a dull shine to the scuffed tile floor. A copy machine hummed in a corner next to a computer grader that looked like a change machine at an arcade.

You had to feed in the answer key first, so the computer would know which answers were right, which were wrong, and the total number of answers. What Mr. Hendrickson didn't realize – or didn't care about – was that I was changing my forms to match the answer key. I was changing Lee's answers, too. I was used to working with tables and charts from the hotel records about which rooms were being rented for how long, so lining up the answer key, my test, and Lee's test, and erasing and filling in appropriately was easy.

At first, I was nervous around Lee. I didn't know what to say or do, so I talked about stupid things. I told her I wanted to be an astronaut.

"You're really smart," Lee said. "I bet you'd be a great astronaut."

"You're really smart, too. You get the same grades I do."

"That's because we're both cheating on the tests."

"Hendrickson has no idea what we're doing in here," I said. Lee opened the refrigerator.

"We could eat his lunch and drink his beer!" she said.

"You know, Lee, I remember when you drank beer in fourth grade and fell asleep."

"Oh yeah," she said, laughing. "My dad mixed up our Thermoses."

"You, you have the most beautiful eyes, Lee," I told her. She smiled.

"Thank you."

"And you've got such a sweet smile, too." Her lips parted, and she ducked her head down like she wanted me to scratch an itchy spot on her scalp. Those were the dumbest, most common things to say, but they worked. I was in.

That night, a power surge reset our alarm clocks, leaving a flashing "EE:EE" in bright red on the numerical faces. I was curled up, straddling my pillow, when I saw a semicircle of light on the ceiling around the chipped light fixture. It was usually still dark when the alarm went off. What time was it?

Panicked, I sat up and looked at the electronic alarm clock on my night stand. "HEE HEE," it read. I dashed to the office in bare feet. The hands of the Marlboro Man clock, which ran on a size-C battery, pointed to 8:21 – 21 minutes after attendance was taken. My mother and I had both overslept.

I ran into my parent's bedroom to wake up my mother.

"Aye, yo, Jesus, my God," she said, pulling on a bathrobe. My father grumbled and turned over on his side. "Get the car keys! They in Daddy's pants pockets!" My father's chinos dangled limply on the stubby bedpost like a lowered flag. I stumbled in the dim light, stepping into a bowl filled with peanut shells that felt like broken glass on my bare feet. I let out a cry of pain and fell to the floor.

"Come on, you stupid! You late for school, you still fooling around! Still hokey pokey around!" my mother yelled. I brushed the shells off my feet. "You go change, I go warm up car," she called after me as I went to my bedroom and pulled on my already-tied sneakers. I was still wearing yesterday's corduroy slacks and a Sea-Shore Linen Supply t-shirt. I could handle the inevitable taunting for wearing the same clothes two days in a row, but my body felt gross. There wasn't even time for me to shower. My hair flopped over like worn-out bristles on an old toothbrush.

I ran to the bathroom sink and threw handfuls of water over my face. Now my hair looked like a worn-out toothbrush that was also wet. I pulled on a Mets sweat-jacket and a Mets baseball cap, both of which had been left by a Benny. On my way out of the office door, I hung up the closed sign and locked the door.

My wet face and neck stung from the cold in the morning air. My breath plumed from my nose and mouth.

My mother was already in the car. A cloud of frozen exhaust materialized beneath our straining Pinto, obscuring the wheels and making it look like a futuristic hovercraft. Then the motor died. My mother frantically jerked the ignition. I couldn't help but laugh at her feeble attempts to start the car.

She got out, her hands pulling the flaps of her bathrobe closed because the belt was missing. "You laughing me? You going walk to school!" she hissed. I didn't know if her teeth were clenched in anger or from the cold.

"Can't I just stay home and say I was sick?"

"No, you going go school! You don't want learn? You lazy?"

"If I walk to school, I'm going to freeze to death!"

"Not so cold!" Our breath mingled and spiraled up.

"It's so cold, the car won't even start!"

"Car didn't sleep late!"

"The power got knocked out!"

"Always have some excuse…you get up same time every day, don't you?"

"You didn't wake up either!"

"I have to work so hard every day, of course I'm tired!" My mother, still in Chinese house slippers, was shifting from foot to foot in a disco-step display of stubbornness to stay out in the cold and argue with her son. My body temperature rose with my anger, and I wasn't feeling the cold anymore.

"I don't get to sleep at night! I rented out two rooms for hookers last night." The words were out. Every letter in H-O-O-K-E-R-S sparkled and pranced in the air like tinsel streamers. My mother took a deep breath and swallowed.

"You going walk to school!" she seethed.

"I'll call a cab."

"They open 9:30."

"Then I'll wait until 9:30."

"You not going wait. You start walking now!"

"I'm going to ask Roy for a ride," I said. My mother gasped.

"You going ride with a black?"

"Why not?"

"You going be killed! They going find your body! You want to die!"

"I'm going to die if I walk!" She fumed. H-O-O-K-E-R-S was still glimmering about two inches away from my mouth.

"Good! Go ride with the black!" My mother stormed to the office. She seemed surprised when she found the door locked. "Stupid kid, you go die!" she called over her shoulder as she fumbled with the keys and unlocked the office door.

I slammed the door to the Pinto and walked to Room 6, where Roy lived. Roy, who looked like he was about 40, was the youngest guy who stayed at the weekly rate. He was also the only non-white at the hotel, besides us.

My mother had two rules: no customers in our living quarters and no renting to blacks.

"Those blacks, they dirty, they steal everything," she explained. I saw only one or two blacks at the hotel a year, and I'd always tell them there were no vacant rooms. They seemed to know what was going on. Roy got to stay because he paid for the entire winter in advance, instead of week to week or hour by hour, like all the other customers.

Roy had been hurt in Vietnam, and he walked by swaying his hips and swinging his legs out in front of him. His head was shaved smooth, and he had a neatly trimmed mustache and beard that looked like velvet against his dark brown skin. It was hard for him to stand straight because of his injury, but he seemed to be of about medium height and build.

Roy stayed in his room working on speeches and poetry most of the time. I could hear the typewriter going sometimes, but I never saw it. The first time I cleaned his room, I was startled. Not by how well-kept it was, but by its bareness. All his belongings were in two padlocked suitcases under the bed. His typewriter and socks – even his razors and shampoo. Another strange thing was that his wastebasket was always empty.

Roy and I didn't talk much, especially compared with the conversations I was forced to have with the white old timers, who were stuffed into the hotel like clothes in storage. If it was an unseasonably warm day, Roy would prop his room door open with the hotel Bible and sit on his chair outside. One day when he was hanging out, he called to me as I was walking back to the office from the school bus stop.

"Hey, what did you learn in school?"

"I learned about the Greeks," I said.

He shrugged and said, "It's all Greek to me!"

Another time, he'd shown me an issue of *Reader's Digest.* They had printed one of his poems.

"Here, read this, tell me what you think," he said. "They paid me $300 for it."

It was a short thing, maybe 10 words long, and it rhymed. It didn't mean anything to me. I forgot it as soon as I read it.

"I...I don't know," I said.

"There's different layers of meaning in poetry," he

said, smiling. "And I guess they missed one of them when they decided to print it! There's different layers of meaning in life, too." He paused. "Now, what are you? You're Chinese, right?"

"I'm an American."

He screwed his face up. "Don't come on like that. I'm an American, too. But I'm black first. Like you're Chinese first."

"I don't know."

"You ever been to China?"

"Nope."

Roy cackled. "I'm a black man, never been to Africa. Never going to Africa. I saw enough in Vietnam and I read enough to know that some of your own kind treat you worse than anyone else. Take advantage of you more than anyone else. Your own kind. Know what I'm saying?" I nodded. I had no idea what he was saying.

He pointed down to the space between his cowboy boots. "This is the best life you can get anywhere. The U.S.A. You can't live anywhere better. That's why your parents came here. If you were in China, you'd be barefoot and stupid for life. Me, too. But you got a place in this country. It isn't always good, but you've got the chance to improve yourself here."

"I want to be an astronaut," I said. He was the first adult I'd told.

"You might have a chance," Roy said, "but you've got to work. You've got to work harder than anybody else. And be very, very lucky. If you really want to be an astronaut, you have to understand the gravity of the situation," he said. "That's a joke," he added when he saw no reaction from me.

I knocked on Roy's door. I heard footsteps inside.

"Roy?" I called through the closed door.

"Oh, it's you." He stumbled to the door and opened it until it caught on the chain lock. Roy shot a look over my head and to both sides. "What's going on?" He didn't sound like he had been sleeping.

"I woke up late but our car won't start and I have to get to school. Can you give me a ride?"

He blinked.

"Yeah, sure," he said. "For you, anything." He shut the door, took off the chain, and opened the door wide. He was dressed in jeans and a sweatshirt.

Roy wobbled down to the driver's side of his Ford Fairlaine and opened the door. He swung into the seat with a motion like a pole vaulter clearing the bar. He snapped the passenger door unlocked, and I got in.

The car was huge. I wondered how it would fit into one lane on the highway. Roy cranked the key and the car started without a problem. It hummed, and I felt the vibration run through my legs and groin.

"You got a girlfriend yet, fellow?" Roy asked. He stroked the velvet on his chin.

"Do you know how to get to the school? I can tell you where to go."

"Oh, don't you go changing the subject! Course I know the way to your school."

"I kinda have a girlfriend, but I haven't even gotten

laid yet." Roy burst out laughing and fell over the steering wheel, but the car never swerved.

"Whoa, good-looking guy like you can't get laid, there's no hope for the rest of us!" He shook his head. "Don't you worry, you still got plenty of time for that yet. Getting laid isn't the end of your problems, it's just the start. Sex complicates life. Keeps you from thinking straight. If I had a girlfriend with me, would I have a poem in *Reader's Digest*? I don't think so."

"I don't want to write poems, I just want to get laid."

"You're gonna learn, you're gonna learn. Lot of guys I knew just wanted to get laid, hanging out all night. When they were in the hospital, though, they just wanted to see their momma one more time before they died. Just wanted to die in their momma's arms."

"I think I hate my mother."

"Now what did you say, fellow?" I saw Roy's grip on the steering wheel tighten. "She raised you, fed you, gave you nice clothes to wear…"

"I found this hat and jacket in one of the hotel rooms," I said.

"You got a hotel. You got a place to live. Lots of people don't have any place to stay, nothing to eat. That's why we have so many wars, because people are hungry. They're fighting so they can eat every day. You have to love your mother. You owe her your life."

"She hates black people," I said. We pulled up to the curb of my school. Roy frowned, then broke into another loud laugh.

"That's okay. I hate Chinese people." There was a

tight smile on his face, but I couldn't tell if he were joking. "Where's your lunch?" he asked, his lips sliding back into neutral. I could feel my stomach grumble, wondering where breakfast was. Roy slipped a Snickers bar into my hands. "Study hard," he said.

When I reached my home room, I couldn't believe my luck. We had a substitute, Mrs. Miller. She hadn't even figured out yet who was in and who was absent. The attendance cards sat in four separate and unequal piles on her desk.

"You, young man, take care of this and I won't count you as late," Mrs. Miller said, waving her hands over the cards. She had huge tits that served as a convenient shelf for her folded arms. But she also had a huge stomach to go with those Dolly Partons.

I surveyed the room. The boys were rapping each other's knuckles with pens. The girls were reading magazines and writing notes to each other. I sorted through the cards and volunteered to take them down to the office.

"I have to take Lee Anderson with me, too. She helps me sort through stuff at the office." Some of the boys made kissy faces and sounds.

"That's enough!" declared Mrs. Miller. That was her two-word phrase. All the subs had one.

Mrs. Griffey would say: "All right!"

Mr. Green: "Settle down!"

Mrs. Schwarz: "People, people!"

The hall monitor waved us through when I showed the attendance envelope. We rounded the corner, and I tried to grab Lee's shoulder. She withdrew and folded her arms.

"Eww, you're wearing the same clothes from yesterday and your hair looks really gross. I think I see bald spots."

"I woke up late, I didn't even have time to shower."

"Eww, scummy boy, I'm never gonna kiss you."

We're going to do more than just kiss, I thought. A lot more.

She was smiling out the side of her mouth.

CHAPTER 11

It was raining when I got off the school bus. I held a three-ring binder over my head as I walked down the long asphalt drive to the hotel office. Our Ford station wagon was gone. The office lights were off and the door was locked. Where had my parents gone? I couldn't remember the last time they'd both left the hotel without telling me. I didn't have the key, so I went to the maid's cart room, pushed aside a few boxes of bulk-packaged cleaning agents, and slipped through a flimsy panel of sheet rock. This led to the back of the refrigerator in the kitchen. I pushed hard, and I was back in our living quarters. I shoved the fridge back against the panel and dumped my books on the table. A box of day-old pastries from Finemann's sat on the counter.

I was hungry, but first things first.

I went into the office, turned on the light, and unlocked the door. I smacked the bell. BING! Open for business. The johns wouldn't come until dark, but some real customers might come in. You never knew.

I ate two apple turnovers standing over the sink, then brushed flakes of pastry and frosting off of my shirt and into the drain. I went into the living room and watched two episodes of "Voltron." My parents were still not back yet.

I took a roll of toilet paper from the bathroom and went to my room. I wrapped my cock up like a little mummy and jerked off to a hard-core magazine with words in German. The woman's head was topped with teased blonde hair, and she was taking his cock in her ass. She must have loved it because she smiled hard – eyes shut, teeth clenched. After I cleaned up, I lay down a little while. When I thought about how tight that girl's asshole must have been, I couldn't sleep. I was hard again.

Afterwards, no one was back yet so I went to the kitchen and scrambled up three eggs with BacOs for dinner. I took two slices of cold wheat bread from the refrigerator and made a sandwich. It was good.

I was washing the frying pan when I looked out the window and saw a figure approaching from the highway. Even from far away, I could tell it wasn't my father or my mother. It was a man in a brown coat and a brimmed hat. I shook off my hands and leaned against the kitchen counter. About three minutes later, I heard the office door open with a small woosh and then the BING!

I went into the office.

The man standing in front of me looked as worn out as his leather coat, which was missing most of its buttons. He was about 50, and his eyes were dull. Droplets of water wiggled on the brim of his hat. I knew he wasn't a john, not only because he didn't have a car, but because he didn't look like a man about to get anything good anytime soon.

He wanted to know how much a room was.

I told him it was $30 for the night.

He didn't say anything, but began to fill out a registration card. I watched him write. I was good at watching people write upside down. He wrote neatly and dotted I's and crossed T's, something I didn't see too often. He left the lines for the driver's license number and car plate blank. I looked over the room schedule and decided to give him Room 7. The man put down the pen.

"That's $30," I said.

He didn't blink or reach for a wallet.

"Thirty dollars," I repeated. He put his hands on the counter and looked at me.

"Can I pay you tomorrow?" he asked.

I shook my head. His bottom lip pushed up against his mouth. His nose twitched, and he sniffed a few times.

"What's that you're cooking?" he asked. Then he muttered to himself, "Eggs."

Now it was my turn to be silent. I looked at him and tried to guess his story. Unemployed and thrown out of his house? Thrown off the train at Asbury Park? He didn't look like he was homeless. Just worn and tired. And hungry.

"God, I haven't eaten all day," he said. I shifted my stance and asked if he was going to pay for the room.

He repeated that he didn't have any money now, but he could pay the next morning. More like he was planning on resting now and running out at dawn.

"I can't rent you a room," I said. He sighed.

"I've been walking around forever. What am I supposed to do?" he said.

"I'll call a cab to take you down to the next hotel," I told him. I called up Seaside Taxi because we used them a lot to take people away, and they were pretty good.

We stood there in the office for about 10 minutes without saying anything to each other. I pretended I was going over the schedule, running my index finger down the list of rooms. The man stood and stared at the Marlboro clock, never taking off his hat, not even stretching.

A car pulled off the highway and drifted down to just in front of the office.

"That's your cab," I told the man. He turned his head and I saw a thin scar on the side of his neck. He made no motion to leave.

"Get in the taxi, please," I told him. "The next hotel is about four miles south on the highway," I added.

He didn't even say thank you. He slowly made his way to the door and then to the cab. He got in and the headlights swept back out to the highway. The brake lights were two sore slitty eyes in the night.

I wondered what the cab driver was going to do when he found out the man couldn't pay.

At about 10 p.m., my parents came home.

"Where did you go?"

"Some business take care," said my father. He was wearing a suit.

"You don't worry about it," said my mother. She gave me a bag from Burger King filled with loose onion rings.

At the bottom was a cold burger. I was already full from the eggs, but I could always go for a burger. I ate it all with a warm glass of iced tea I made from a powder mix. Now that they were back, I could go out and clean rooms.

I picked up two buckets filled with cleaning supplies and headed out.

All of our relatives lived in Taiwan, except for a distant cousin of my father who'd moved to Los Angeles. The Taiwan relatives shipped boxes of clothes for me that were about three sizes too small and stank from being packed with jars of Chinese medicine and creams. The one pair of socks that did fit smelled of Tiger Balm even after several washings. The L.A. cousin sent us seedless oranges.

We got word one day that the L.A. cousin wanted to visit. My father brought him and his wife back from Newark airport in the Pinto. They looked shocked and horrified as they stepped into our living quarters. Uncle and Aunty, as I was told to address them, were wearing nice shoes that looked as out of place on our shabby carpeting as a shaky fish fin on dry land for the first time. They probably expected bellhops running around, mint chocolates on the pillows, and a spacious lobby swirling in Muzak. The only thing we had that made us a legitimate hotel was the BING! BING! BING!

"You stay in Room 2," my mother told me. "Uncle and Aunty going stay in your room." I nodded. They were all going out to some Chinese restaurant the next town over. I had to stay to watch the office, so I fried two eggs and baked some biscuits for dinner.

I didn't get a good look at Aunty until they came back from the restaurant and she took her coat off. Were her tits small. They weren't even big enough to cast a shadow.

The adults went into the kitchen and my father took out a white ceramic bottle from the top shelf of the cabinet.

"Go into Room 2," he said. "We watch the office now." In the air there was a sense of politeness under pressure. It smelled like Tiger Balm.

I went into the hotel room, sat on the bed, and turned on the television. "Barney Miller" was on 11, the only channel that came in well. I heard some shouting. At first, I thought it was coming from one of the other rooms, but it continued, and I picked up some Chinese. The women were louder than the men. Then it stopped for a while.

A few minutes later, a Seaside Taxi pulled up to the office and honked twice. I went to the window. Uncle carried all the luggage out the door, staggering and grunting. After heaving the suitcases into the trunk, he shook a fist back at the office and shouted, then high kicked into the air like he was going for an extra point. Aunty's head sagged with disappointment and embarrassment. She touched a hand to her hair before stepping into the cab. Then they were gone.

I went into the office and saw both my parents with their arms folded, standing behind the counter. Their faces were red from alcohol and from arguing.

"What happened?" I asked.

"Nothing," my father said.

"They had emergency," my mother said.

"Can I sleep in my room tonight?"

"Yes," said my mother. "You clean up everything in Room 2 first."

"Where did they go?"

"They all get in argument. Stupid argument."

"Not stupid argument. Serious argument," said my father.

"Stupid," said my mother.

"I'm not going to say nothing if someone wants to say bad things about Chinese people. Mainland people are our countrymen! We support them."

"You never even been to China, how you know them? How you know they won't attack Taiwan?"

I didn't know what was more incredible – that my parents were arguing or that they were doing it in English in front of me.

"I don't have to go to China to know them! I worked with mainland people at my job."

"You don't have job anymore!"

"My job is fixing hotel!"

"I never see you work!"

"Come down to basement!"

"You don't want be near me anymore." My mother was crying. My father put his arm around her. That was where the English stopped.

Thanksgiving weekend at the hotel was a depressing place to be. Commercials on television showed relatives coming together at a table set with pumpkin pie, cranberry sauce, mincemeat, and other things I'd only seen at the supermarket. Kitchens and dining rooms bustling with children and a playful golden retriever. A crackling fireplace. Brassy music. And lots of love. Heaps of it.

All we had on Thanksgiving was a puny turkey. It sucked even more because instead of eating in front of the TV, I had to sit with my mother and father at the dining table. Cup-ring stains on the kitchen table in front of my father looked like the Olympics logo. The turkey was so dry, it crumbled like mummy meat as my father cut away at it. There was also rice, hot chili sauce, and string beans. Great.

I mushed all the ingredients together in my bowl, and surprisingly it didn't taste too bad. I used chopsticks, too, but I had to use a fork for the string beans. I was going to head to the fridge to grab a Briardale cola for myself when I heard the office door open. Then heavy footsteps. Two seconds later: BING! BING! BING!

I swung open the office door and saw a man in a big puffy winter coat. A Yankees cap was pulled just over his eyebrows.

"I need a room for a few hours," he said in a gruff voice.

"That's $20."

"C'mon, it's Thanksgiving."

"It's always $20."

"All right, I know how you Filipinos are," he said, reaching for his wallet. "You know, we fought in your country. We protected your people. We drove the Spanish out. But business is always business with you."

He sighed as he pulled out a twenty. It was folded in half, and he placed it on the counter so it stood on its edge. That bill was standing straight and tall for the pride of America. Pilgrim's pride. The fold went right through Andrew Jackson's face.

"You have to fill out the registration card."

"I'm just here for a little while, come on!" A wave of nausea washed over me as the man's beer-marinated breath blasted out.

"Just put your name down."

"That's how it is, that's how it always is. Fucking Filipinos. Shit." He hesitated, thinking up a name, then scrawled it in. He turned the clipboard to me and tapped his handwriting. "You happy, kid? That do it for you?" I nodded my head, handing him the key to Room 5. "Now do the both of us a favor," the man said, working the key into his tight back pocket, "and wipe that mouth, okay?" He turned and left.

I shook my head and read the name again. I would have thought Mr. Hendrickson could have come up with something better than "John Smith."

That's when I realized that despite everything, I loved being behind the front desk. People did what I told them to. The President could come in and he wouldn't get a room until he filled out a card and paid me.

The hotel was a prison, but at least I was the top dog. Nobody came through until I got my bite.

CHAPTER 12

It was December and the birds didn't sing. Lonely old men stayed in their rooms, fiddling with the television reception. The sun never shone through the cloud cover that would roll in from the ocean. You looked at your watch and looked up to the sky, and you couldn't tell if it was a.m. or p.m. The light that did trickle down turned everything a heavy gray. I was sleepy when I went to bed and sleepy when I got up.

The few johns that came in lacked enthusiasm, acting like they were tossing pocket change at a pay-toll basket. They were a far cry from the anxious and sweaty men with shaky hands who practically humped the counter in the warmer months.

I wasn't feeling so hot to get laid now either. I'd read a joke about having to eat smelly pussies in the January issue of *Gent,* and it sort of churned my stomach when I thought of Lee Anderson finally opening her legs to me.

Then there was December 7th. I used to worry about that. I heard "jap" a lot on television, backed by black-and-white film. I guess that's where the other kids heard it, too. When they started tagging me with it, I took it as them calling me "fag" and took care of them accordingly.

Vincent had taught me how to dish out shit when I had to.

"You ever knock a guy down," said Vincent, pointing at the soft skin above my nose and between my eyes, "start jumping on him. Jump on his fucking knees and ankles, man. He'll never walk right again." I was already bigger than most of the other kids, but it never hurt to know how to shove the knobby end of your wrist into the throat or how to bring that knee into the gut. No one called me "jap" or just plain "chink" anymore to my face.

"Why did the Japanese bomb Pearl Harbor?" I asked my mother once.

"Japanese, they were so cruel. They kill Chinese, burn some of them alive," she said. "They fight on same side as Nazis."

"How come the racists were on the same side as Japan?"

"Because they wanted to help Japan attack China and kill Chinese."

"Their country is so small, how could they attack China?"

"Chinese fighting with each other."

"Why were they fighting each other? You told me Chinese people were smart."

"Chinese are smartest people in whole world."

"Then why did they turn communist?" My mother sighed and waved the question away like it was a hungry mosquito.

"Don't ask me that now. I have to clean rooms. Go do your homework."

"I did my homework already. I'm taking care of the office now."

"Then take care office."

"I'm already here."

"I'm going to clean rooms," she said again, heading for the cleaning cart. "Don't rent Room 6. Smells really bad. I think we have to shampoo rug."

Christmas vacation found me in a lethargy, fat from overeating and lack of business at the hotel. My mother gave me extra money when I went to the hardware store so I could pick up some stuff from Finemann's Thrift Bakery on the way home. Maybe a cake or pie could add some holiday cheer to the season.

They didn't do any baking at the thrift "bakery," but it smelled wonderful. Finemann's actual bakeries were located up and down the Jersey shore, and at the end of the day, what each store hadn't been able to sell would be trucked over to the thrift bakery. That was the law, the woman at the counter told me when I asked why the apple pies were only a dollar apiece.

"My darling little Chinese boy," she said, rubbing my head and tugging my ears like she was peeling fruit. Jesse, as her name tag read, was about 30 years old with a fiery red swirl of hair. "It's so good to see you again. Do you celebrate the holidays?"

"We celebrate Christmas."

Jesse tilted her head slightly.

"And how did that happen? You're Chinese, aren't you? Don't you have those holidays with the firecrackers and the dragon dances? You know. That rich, oriental heritage?"

"I'm an American."

"Well, you really came from somewhere else, now didn't you?" Jesse's questions reminded me of the first day of school of every year of my life. If she were a boy about my age, I would've broken her face. But she was no boy. Jesse's breasts were ample enough to palm like the pointy ends of two Nerf footballs. Her waist was strangely small for where she worked. Her face was flabby, though. It reminded me of a roll of biscuit dough that had expired and oozed through the diagonal seams of the cardboard can. Other than that, she was a pretty damned sexy slut.

"I'm just looking for some Christmas cookies or cakes," I said.

"Well, we don't have any. This is a Jewish bakery," she said, blushing, which made her face look a little better.

Jesse tried to push fluffy, fruity things on me, but I really wanted something heavy and chocolate.

I picked up three pounds of brownies, or what looked like brownies, for $1.25. On the way out, Jesse rubbed my ears again, but gently – even sensually – this time.

"No hat or ear muffs in this cold! And you need a new coat! You're gonna freeze out there like a little bald Buddha!" she said.

"I'll be okay," I said, switching the heavy sack of salt rock from the hardware store to under my left armpit. When I got on my bike, I balanced the sack on the handlebars and put the box of brownies on top.

On my way home, I had to go around some icy puddles that had formed at the side of the highway. Parts of the roads fell apart in the winter. Our town only patched things up for the Bennys.

I put the brownies on the kitchen table. No one was home again. My mother was nowhere to be seen, and the light in my father's workshop was off.

The kitchen walls were sparsely covered with Christmas cards. Most were from our institutional suppliers and had rubber-stamped signatures. The linen company, the detergent and soaps company, and the locksmiths. Three dark red and gold cards were marked with nervous Chinese scribbles, but I had no idea who'd sent them. The only word they had in English was my name at the top.

I went into the office and sat down behind the front desk. I looked at the calendar under the Marlboro clock and counted the days left in my vacation. Ten and a half. Business at the hotel was at its slowest this time of year. Because of the proximity of Jesus' birth, johns were reluctant to come to the hotel. They were probably at home with their wives, kids, and newly bought presents. The odd john or two who would stagger in each day were the ugliest things you'd ever seen. They probably had nobody at home and no one to buy gifts for. Shame rippled in their eyes when they looked up.

Looking at them, I couldn't help but think that maybe I'd be a john someday. I already had no home and no one I really wanted to buy presents for. Maybe I'd get so desperate to just fuck that I really would end up on the other side of the counter. Years and years from now, I'd be staying here at the weekly rate with the other washed-up men.

Living in these hotel rooms was the worst thing I could imagine. Sleeping on old comestains. Looking at myself everyday in a medicine-cabinet mirror that had cracked from being slammed shut too many times. Keeping my clothes in a desk drawer with a Bible at the bottom. Watching TV with one hand on the antenna because it made the reception better. All that was in my future, assuming I couldn't find a way out.

Our living quarters right now weren't great, but they were a hell of a lot better than the hotel rooms. I was already sleeping on old comestains, though.

I stayed in the office for a little bit, rocking back and forth on the barstool. I opened the cash drawer and fingered the change bin, looking for pennies with wheat stalks on the back. I had a peanut-butter pail filled with them. They were minted from 1909 to 1958 and were worth a lot more than coins with the Lincoln Memorial on the reverse. Also, the U.S. mint redesigned the obverse on the later coins, lowering the profile of Lincoln's bust to make it less subject to wear and tear. I'd found this out from a coin magazine with a feature on penny collecting. I'd studied the chart next to the article, and after a while, I'd memorized the years and mint marks of the scarcest pennies. I was constantly looking for them whenever I came across any change. There was no way the 1955 doubled-die error would get by me.

Positive that no one would walk into the office for at least the next 15 minutes, I snuck back to my room. I flipped through *Busty Bitches In Heat*, a hard-core magazine. It had still been shrink-wrapped with a "3 For $9.99" sticker when Crispy gave it to me. The pages smelled funny, like ripe bananas, and I had to fold them down to keep the magazine open. I looked at the last page and wondered if cocks tasted as bad as pussy. It was all skin, and not wet, so maybe it didn't. How did come taste? I never wanted to taste my own because it smelled like salty bathroom cleaner.

I was stroking hard when I heard BING! BING! BING!

"Shit, motherfucker!" I said, slipping the magazine into the pillowcase. A john was in the office. This one was different from the others, though.

For one thing, he was dressed in a blue button-down shirt and a sports jacket. All the johns I'd seen before had on t-shirts or big coats that covered even their Adam's apple.

"Do I have to fill out a card?" he asked.

"Please," I said.

"Isn't this enough of an ID?" he said, opening his wallet. There was a police badge inside. The shine was a lot duller than I thought it should be. "How do you like that for a fucking ID?" he asked quietly. He made no motion to fold up the wallet.

I'd been expecting this day for quite a while now. The cops had probably had one or more undercover guys renting out our rooms the previous week to check out the operation. What was going to happen to me? Since I was a minor, they couldn't charge me with anything. Maybe they'd haul off my parents for endangering the welfare of a child, though. The cops were going to ransack our files, then slit our mattresses and empty the pillowcases so that they could look for drugs or counterfeit money.

When they found my magazines, they'd say, "Look at this little pervert! Can't get laid so he wacks off!" They'd have a few rounds of laughter over that.

I looked at the badge again. It looked like the fender of a car that had just hit me. The man finally closed the wallet and put it away.

"I should get this room for free," he said. "The other guys get better places than this for free. I'm here because it's the closest hotel right now. Why the fuck they got a little kid to run this joint is beyond me." I swallowed and slipped him the key to Room 4.

"You adopted or something? Were your parents killed in Vietnam?"

"I'm an American," I said. He was smiling now.

"Was your dad a soldier or something? Knocked up a little mama-san?"

I must have looked like I was ready to cry.

"I'm only going to be about an hour," he said, dangling the key like a metal lure.

He turned and was walking away when he suddenly stepped back and dropped a bill on the counter. "You people have Christmas, too, don't you?" he said. The bill had been rolled up and then flattened, like a stepped-on cigarette. I didn't know it was a twenty until after he was gone, when I unrolled it.

My parents came in later that night. My father was in a suit again. My mother was wearing a nice dress with light jewelry. I was used to seeing him in a ratty sweater over a wrinkled undershirt. She usually had on wash-worn sweatpants and a sweatjacket.

"Where have you been?" I asked.

"We brought back Chinese food," my mother said, brandishing a bag that bulged with boxy containers.

"You know I can't eat…" I began.

"I get a lot of sweet-and-sour pork for you," she said. That was the only Chinese food I could take.

"Where did you go?" I asked my father.

"Some business take care," he grunted.

I opened the box of fried pork chops and sat in front of the television. A "Happy Days" rerun was on. Arnold was going, "Bah hah hah, Richie! Bah hah hah!" His wide, flat face was pulled back as if someone had him by the hair. It reminded me of what I looked like when I stepped out of the shower and squeezed zits from my chin onto the mirror.

Two days later, on Christmas Eve, I unwrapped a present from my mother and father – a pack of six men's crew socks that my big feet could grow into. My present from Santa Claus, which bore the same tag and hand-writing as the present from my parents, was a Mattel Electronics hand-held football game.

I gave my mother the biggest box of turtle chocolates they had at the supermarket. I gave my father an Indestrukt rubber mallet so he wouldn't leave impressions of the hammer head in the wood anymore. He'd already split a few door frames with his rusty metal hammer. They both knew I didn't have an allowance and that I'd taken money from the cash drawer in the office to buy the presents. But they smiled and said thanks. Was that love?

That vacation, my father wanted to watch some big football games on television, so I couldn't play Atari. I ended up taking a nine-volt battery from his calculator and hooking it up to the little football game I'd gotten from Cheap Chinese Claus. I knew the game was marked down because I saw the store circular in the Sunday newspaper. Mattel Electronics Football 2 had just been released, and the original Mattel Electronics Football units were slashed down to $2.99. They were less than half the price of the cheapest Atari cartridges, which were what I'd really wanted.

Playing the football game was like watching little radioactive fleas jumping five yards at a time. The flea carrying the ball glowed brighter than the others. After playing for half an hour, you'd see gray after-images of all those dots jumping around when you looked up at the ceiling. This must be what it's like to be high, I thought. I switched the game off and went to my room to read more letters to *Velvet*.

The following Sunday, there was a small item in the paper about a trial where a girl said she'd been gang-raped in one of our rooms. My parents were mentioned as the proprietors of the hotel who had testified for the defense.

CHAPTER 13

BING! BING! BING! It was about seven in the morning on December 29th. I walked into the office and was taken aback by the number of people waiting at the counter. First, I noticed the man with the badge. Then the absurdly fat man and woman. The tubby kid, Mitchell Cone, was someone I already knew. He had about two years and a hundred pounds on me, although we were in the same grade. Despite Mitchell's rep as a bully, he was looking pale and weak now. Nothing close to skinny, though.

The man with the badge leaned his elbows on the counter.

"Are your parents around? Mommy and Daddy home?" he asked, looking down at me. I looked at his badge, which read, "SHERIFF." I was wearing my gray sweatpants and my feet were bare. A tattered plaid shirt that I'd grown accustomed to wearing to bed hung on my shoulders.

"Do you need a room?" I asked, looking the sheriff in the eyes and sitting on the barstool. I placed my hands on my side of the counter and straightened up. It was obvious that I was familiar with working the desk. The sheriff coughed and hooked a thumb into his belt.

"These people have been evicted from their property. Do you have any efficiency rooms?"

"We have rooms with two burning hotplates and a small refrigerator. We don't provide any cooking ware or utensils," I said.

"They've got pots and pans, so that's all right," he said. "Now folks, let's get your stuff out of my car."

Mr. Cone filled out the registration card. He was wearing a grimy blue winter coat.

"How long will you be staying?" I asked.

"I don't know. Could be a few months. Do you have a discount for month to month?"

"No, $60 a week is as low as I can go." He grimaced, but paid for the first two weeks. I marked it down in the books.

Everything the Cone family owned fit into three plastic garbage bags. A high heel poked out of one of the bags. An electric plug tore a hole out of another. I gave Mr. Cone the key to Room 8 and watched the fatsos waddle out of the office. Room ate. Now that was funny. I smirked, and Mitchell turned his head and caught it.

"I guess we'll be taking the bus together, Mitchell," I said. Some color came back into his face as he flipped me off.

Mitchell and I found ourselves together by default; neither of us had any friends around. The kids I knew from school said their parents wouldn't drive them over to the hotel, which was isolated from the good residential neighborhoods by the four-lane interstate. The concrete bunker and chain link fence on the divider made the interstate look like the Berlin Wall.

Mitchell didn't have any friends because at one time or another, he'd beaten up half of the school – all the boys. He even hung out with the intermediate school burnouts.

I'd first met Mitchell at the start of the previous year when I was at the water fountain. He'd body-slammed into me, knocking my head around like a pinball stuck between rubber bumpers. Ready to kick some ass, I yanked my head out and shook off my hair. The first thing I saw was what looked like a teenager with a beer belly.

"Fucking Charlie Chan, don't you even know how to get a drink? You need a pair of chopsticks or something?" Mitchell was a half foot taller and a foot wider than me. His dark brown hair drooped down in tangled strands over his eyes and ears. Two of his scabby fists were already raised to my face.

I kicked his shins, but that didn't do anything, and I ended up on the hallway floor. He spat at my feet before turning and walking away. The school soccer trophies in the case next to me never looked taller.

Mitchell might have killed somebody if he'd attended school regularly, but he only showed up two or three times a week. When he was in school, he was constantly shuttled from classroom to guidance counselor to the principal's office. More than a few times, he'd walk straight out the school's front door, just to save a few steps.

After my first brush with him, I Krazy-Glued the combination dial of his locker, but I was never rewarded with seeing him pound away at the metal door. Maybe he didn't even use his locker.

This year, Mitchell was supposed to be in my class, but he hadn't made it in since school began. On the first day, Mr. Hendrickson flipped through the attendance cards, assigned seats, noted faces. When Mitchell's name was called, feet shuffled nervously with the realization that he'd been left behind again, and that he would be sitting amongst us.

Mitchell had been marked absent, but he was assigned a desk at the end of a row. The boy seated to the left of Mitchell's desk squirmed in his chair every morning, anticipating the imminent arrival of pain. But Mitchell didn't come in late that day, or any other.

Eavesdropping from the living room into the hotel office and piecing together what my mother told me later, I managed to get the story. Mitchell's father had told my mother all about his lousy luck and his lousy kid, trying to wrangle a lower room rate with his sob story. Of course he didn't get one.

Mitchell's father used to work for a home-building company further up the shore. His specialty was hammering deck planks together and waterproofing the wood. Business was good once, but had fallen off after medical waste had started washing up. The company told him they'd call when they had work. He wasn't cut off completely, but the $25 a week the company paid him to stay home wasn't going to cover the rent, much less the installments on the car he'd bought to commute to the job he no longer had.

He stayed at home with his wife, eating and watching TV and trying to stay off the phone. They wondered what Mitchell was learning in school, but were afraid to ask. Mitchell got grouchy whenever they brought it up.

The phone was the first thing that was cut off. Then the gas. They fell half a year behind in the rent. They never answered the door anymore. Then, just as summer began, they came home from a movie and found a notice from the bank saying that they were going to repossess the car. They threw everything into the trunk and drove their Duster south to his mother-in-law's place in Nashville.

After a while, Mitchell's father managed to find a job with another home builder. Mitchell was bored living in a town with nothing to do, so he begged his father to take him to work that first day. Mitchell stayed inside the new house as his father hammered out planks for the porch and pool deck. A vandal at heart, Mitchell was caught kicking out the spokes of a wooden staircase on the second floor by the couple visiting their future home. Both Mitchell and his father were thrown off the property that same first day of work. They hadn't even made it to lunch break.

Mitchell's grandmother eventually got fed up with the freeloaders on her living-room floor. She woke them up early one Friday morning and told them they had to go after breakfast. Then she made some pancakes. The Cones came back to Jersey and called up the sheriff to get their stuff back from the house. But the bank had already repossessed all the furniture and sold it off.

The school-bus stop was at the end of the hotel's drive-way, right at the edge of the interstate. Cars on both sides had to stop when the school bus flashed its lights and picked us up. That pissed the commuters off. I tried to board the bus as quickly as possible, because I didn't want the drivers to gawk too long at the poor Chinese kid who lived at the shabby hotel. We owned the place, but standing out in front like that, I looked like I belonged in one of the rooms. Son of a whore. Poor Amerasian refugee. Little beggar boy by the highway.

I liked the winter better because I could pull down the hood of my winter jacket and tighten the drawstrings, making my face disappear. Only my nose would show.

On the first day back to school after Christmas, I was waiting at the stop, pulling my hood loose so I could make it tighter. My lips were bleeding where the skin had dried and cracked. I drew a layer of Chap Stick over my lips and smacked them.

A large lumpy figure in a denim jacket shuffled down to the bus stop. Mitchell wasn't carrying anything. No book bag, no books, no lunch. He wasn't even wearing mittens. His bare hands flexed at his sides as if he were squeezing the cold out of them. Mitchell's hair hung in oily, shaggy layers. When he got close enough, he said, "Did I just see you put on some lipstick, you little faggot?"

"It was Chap Stick."

"Yeah, I know that, chinkie. I was just joking. I'm trying to lighten up the mood around here. It's embarrassing enough that I gotta wait here with you."

"Don't you need a notebook?"

"The fuck for? If it's already in the book, why should I write it down again? Doesn't make any fucking sense." He unzipped his jacket, reached in, and pulled out a dented cigarette. Mitchell stuck it in his mouth and his hands dove into his coat pockets like fat gophers jumping back into their holes. "Fuff!" he groaned as the cigarette wiggled in his mouth.

Mitchell yanked out the cigarette. "You gotta match?" he asked me. I shook my head. "Course not, fucking chinkie," he muttered, shoving the cigarette into his back pants pocket.

The bus stopped with a groan and the door swung open.

"Brainiacs first," said Mitchell, sweeping his arms to the door. I was a brainiac because I hadn't been left back. I stepped up and worked my way down the aisle over feet, book bags, and trombones. Boys hunched over their bleeping electronic sports games, and girls read *Seventeen* together. I wondered if Mitchell was going to sit with me behind the hump seat – the one just above the rear wheel. If you sat in the two rows behind it, you were cool. But you had to be tough. If there was someone sitting in my back seat, I'd pull them out by the neck of their coat. Maybe Mitchell would pull me out.

I heard the driver yelling. I stopped in the aisle and turned around.

"Get off my bus!" Mrs. Krackowski yelled at Mitchell. She knew Mitchell because he'd beaten up her son Matt, who was a year younger than me. She stood at the top of the boarding steps, arms jutting out in sharp angles from her rounded body.

"I'm going to school!" Mitchell yelled back.

"Is this your stop? Where's your bus pass?"

"I don't have a pass! I just moved back two days ago!"

"You don't have a pass, you don't get on my bus! Now get off!" She roared like a well-fed furnace, blowing Mitchell back onto the hotel's driveway. She hopped back into the driver's seat and slammed the doors shut.

"Fuck you, fat, ugly bitch!" Mitchell yelled. You could hear him with the doors and all the windows shut. He gave a double bird as we pulled away.

I felt a little bad for him. Mitchell was just trying to go to school. Granted, his record spoke for itself, but he never got a chance to set it straight. He'd already had a pretty shitty life. And now he was living at our hotel, something no kid deserved, no matter how bad they were.

The next day, Mitchell was back at the bus stop with a yellow bus pass that was already crumpled and creased like a brown paper bag over a whisky flask.

"That fucking bitch-fuck, the pass didn't come in the mail until yesterday. I should sue her for keeping me outta school." He lit up a cigarette and flicked the match away. It was even colder than the day before. My breath was as thick as his smoke in the air. We didn't say anything for a while, just stood there watching my breath and his smoke.

"What grade are you going to be in?" I asked.

"I don't know. I don't how many years they're going to leave me back, now." Mitchell's shoulders rose up and down like ocean waves in a storm as he laughed. "I don't even know what grade I'm supposed to be."

"Where's your lunch?" I asked.

"They sent me a slip for that, too. They give me lunch." He was one of the kids taking the cheese and mustard sandwiches handed out by the janitor's office. On Fridays, they got apples, too.

When the bus came, Mitchell held his arm out. "Let me get on first," he said. He slipped the bus pass between his fingers so the middle one stuck out in front.

"Here's my pass, Krackowski!" he shouted at her. Then he waved it to the rest of the kids on the bus. They roared with laughter. Mitchell Cone was back. Mrs. Krackowski stomped her foot and yelled for him to take a seat. She nearly took my leg off when she slammed the bus door shut.

I plopped down in the front seat next to Crispy.

"Hey!" Mitchell yelled from the back. "Hey, get over here! Sit here, man!" he was patting the next-to-last seat right in front of him. The boy sitting in it immediately scooted out. When I sat down, I knew I was Mitchell's friend.

"I can't believe I'm going back to this shitty school. I wish I could just drop out and work on houses like my dad. It's easy. You could do it. I could be making tons of money, but I have to waste my whole day at school. I'm not learning shit, anyway."

He spotted a boy with Mattel Electronics Football 2.

"Hey, lemme try that!" Mitchell pointed a finger at the game and nodded to me. That finger looked like three little linked sausages. I held my hand out and got the game and gave it to Mitchell. He gave it back later, but not until we pulled into the school.

The sea of kids parted before Mitchell and me. Boys and girls darted to the sides of the hallway, their eyes big like frightened fish on nature shows trying to get away from the camera. We parted ways when Mitchell went into the office to hammer out a schedule. Lee Anderson came up to me at my locker.

"Why are you hanging out with that asshole Mitchell?" she asked.

"I'm not. He lives at our hotel now. We wait at the bus stop together," I said.

"I thought he moved away."

"He's back. His family lost their house. I think the government is giving them money to stay at our hotel." She chewed on her lips, leaving a red lipstick stain on her teeth. She could probably give a damn good blow job.

"Why do you have to hang out with him? You're such a smart guy." I was wishing she wasn't holding her books across her tits so I could feel them press against me. Instead, I had to settle for her thigh against mine. It felt soft and warm.

There was a slap at the back of my head. It was Mitchell.

"Hey, put your dick away! I'm in your class, so show me how to get to there," he said.

As drawn as I was to Lee, I couldn't help but look away to

see what Mitchell was doing in class. Rapping other kids' knuckles with his pencil. Folding a page in his textbook over and over so it looked like a Chinese fan. Well-timed facial expressions and exaggerated yawns. I knew Mitchell was a bad kid, but he was damned funny to watch.

Too bad it didn't last the whole year. He never came back after that week. Instead, he stayed in the hotel room, watching TV.

One day, after a heavy snowfall, he waited for me to get off the bus and nailed me with a snowball right in the face when I was on the last step. It hit me so hard I heard a buzzing sound in my right ear. I picked up a hunk of brown slush stained with car exhaust and hurled it at him, but it went over his head.

I chased him up the drive, but giddiness and slipping on the ice slowed me down. This was my first snowball fight against another person. I used to throw snowballs at trailer trucks on the highway, but that wasn't really a fight. I tossed my books by the swimming-pool fence.

Mitchell's hands were bare, so he could pack snowballs tighter and harder than I could with the worn-out work gloves I wore as mittens. I picked up a trash-can lid and used it as a shield. Mitchell did the same. We charged each other. I was holding a chunk of ice that must have weighed 10 pounds. I crowned Mitchell with it before he had a chance to block it. Stunned, he stumbled back and fell. For a moment, a flap of blubber slipped out from under his t-shirt.

Suddenly, Mitchell was on his feet and in my face. I turned, but fell into a snow drift. Again and again, he smacked his trash-can lid into my head. Something sharp was gouging out my scalp, but it didn't hurt because of the cold.

When he stopped he said, "Holy fuck, man, you're bleeding!" I touched my glove to my forehead and it came away slick and dark. I looked at the lid, now frozen in Mitchell's hand. The ends of the bolts that held the lid handle in place were bloody.

"Shit!" grunted Mitchell. He picked up handfuls of snow powder and rubbed it into my head. I sat up, looking at my bloody glove for a minute. My hands were empty...what was I carrying...school...

"My books...I need my books," I said. Getting back on my feet felt like climbing a rubber ladder. Mitchell went back and hastily grabbed my books. I staggered back to the office, one hand on my head and the other in front of my face. The wound didn't hurt at all, but I was feeling cold and dizzy. We got back into the office, and I let Mitchell come into our living quarters behind the front desk – the first customer ever to do so.

My mother was sitting on the couch, watching a soap opera.

"Blood! What happen! Blood!" she blurted.

"I fell down," I said, sinking into a chair. Mitchell dumped my books onto the floor at my feet.

"He slipped and fell," Mitchell said, looking around the living room. "Hey, you got Atari!" he said. My mother glared at him, and he shrugged and left.

"You so careless, play too rough," she said. She went downstairs and came back with my father and a wet towel.

"Look what your son did," she said, wrapping my head with the towel. "Look what he did." My mother was talking like I'd broken a vase.

"You okay?" my father asked. "What happen?"

"He playing rough with fat boy!" my mother snapped.

Just then, someone charged into the office and rang the bell, BING! BING! BING! My mother abandoned me and popped into the office.

"I saw it all. That fat white kid just slammed your son into the ground," I heard Roy growl.

"I know," said my mother in a voice that sounded more shocked by the appearance of an angry black man in the office than by my bloody face.

"I'm going to talk to that fat kid's parents," said Roy. "They have to show that kid some direction. I suggest you do the same with yours." The front door swung in what sounded like a wide arc before shutting.

"I fell," I said softly. My father shook his head.

"Better calm down, or else you lose more blood," he said. After about an hour, the bleeding stopped.

BING! BING! BING! went the office bell. My mother was taking a nap and my father was back in the workshop, so I closed my book and went into the office. It was Mitchell's mother.

"I saw the blood in the snow, and Mitchell told me you fell down. Are you okay?" she asked. I nodded and waved my hand.

Something smelled meaty. Mitchell's mother was holding our casserole dish. It was stuffed with pasta, sausage and cheese.

"And this is your dish back, thank you for lending it to us," she said. "You tell your mother an American never returns a dish empty." She was smiling, but the expression on her face was condescending, like she was granting us a favor instead of returning one.

The fact was, they were two weeks behind in the rent.

"Are you paying the rent?" I asked quietly, looking into her eyes. "It's late." She reddened a bit and gently pushed the dish across the counter.

"Jim's still looking for a job. He'll find one soon," she said. "We've already talked to your mother about that."

"Okay," I said. Dodging lenders was one thing for Mrs. Cone, but dodging me was another matter. How embarrassing it must have been to have to answer to a 12-year-old kid. A 12-year-old chink.

They must have left in the night.

On my way to the school-bus stop the next day, I saw that their car was gone. I went up to their room and saw that the shades were thrown wide open. They'd stripped the pillows and sheets from the bed. The towels were probably also gone. I cupped my hands to the window and swept my eyes across the room.

They'd taken the television, too.

Mitchell's family had hit the road, bound for some other place that would take them in for a while. The father was trained in building homes, but he couldn't find one for his own family.

CHAPTER 14

There was a hurricane on Groundhog Day. The entire hotel whistled and moaned as the wind blew through it. The skies were bruised gray and purple. Clouds were tight, thin strands of cotton candy that sped by like time-lapse photography.

I was in the kitchen scrambling eggs and listening to the radio to see if school was going to be canceled. I'd already showered and changed, but I was ready to head back to sleep if it was.

Two local school districts had already been closed so far, but not mine.

Oil splattered against the cuff of my polyester dress shirt. I'd inherited a number of the shirts my father used to wear when he was a civil engineer in New York City. They were thin and didn't offer much warmth, but they made you sweat where the fabric touched your skin. My father now preferred wearing t-shirts, since his workshop was next to the boiler room. He was dressed like a kid all day while I was wearing a men's shirt with a tag on the collar that read "14-28."

Three more districts canceled school.

I shook some BacOs into the pan, stirred it a little, and turned off the heat. I slid the egg into my plate, but before I started eating, I washed off the spatula and pan. I opened the door to the toaster oven, stabbed both pieces of toast with my fork and dragged them onto my eggs.

I'd just finished eating and was washing my plate and fork when it was announced that my school would also be closed.

I went back to my bedroom and pulled off my clothes. I read a few letters in *Mayfair*, but I was feeling sleepy and couldn't get hard. My stomach was warm, and fats and oils were seeping through my body, slowing everything down.

I knew I was dreaming right away because school was canceled, but there I was in class. I was in my seat, but the other students were gone. A figure was slumped over in the teacher's seat. The hurricane roared on. Outside the classroom windows, bare trees in the school yard were pulled back like slingshots by the onslaught of wind and water.

The teacher sat up. It wasn't Mr. Hendrickson.

It was my father.

He was wearing a t-shirt and briefs.

"You ready?" he asked me.

"Ready for what?"

"You like singing, don't you?"

"Not really."

"You like songs, don't you?"

"Yes."

"You're going to like this song. You already know the words!"

Kookaburra sits in the old gum tree
Merry merry king of the bush is he
Laugh, kookaburra, laugh, kookaburra
Save some gum for me

It was a song I learned in third grade. What was a kookaburra? It was a bird. What was a gum tree? I still didn't know.

"Sing it with me!" yelled my father. His accent was gone, and he was strangely loose. I started to sing with him.

"Kookaburra sits in the old..."

"No!"

"Kookaburra sits..."

"No! No!"

"Kooka..."

"Stop! I start first! You wait until I hit the next line and then you start. You know what that's called? It's called singing in rows! I'll start now, are you ready?"

"Yes."

"Kookaburra sits in the old gum tree..."

"Kookaburra sits in the old gum tree..." He sang "Laugh, kookaburra, laugh, kookaburra," when I sang, "Merry merry king of the bush is he."

"That's right," he said as I finished up. "Do you get it?"

"Yes, I understand."

"You sing the same exact song as me, word for word,

only you're one line behind. You're always one line behind me."

"I know."

"It's the same song!" he yelled, picking up a hammer and throwing it at the window.

At the sound of the crash, I jumped out of bed. My window was wide open, and I stood on my night table and latched it shut. Raindrops splattered against the glass as if it were the windshield of a speeding car.

Even the johns stayed away from the hotel in February. Maybe something about Valentine's Day and sticking with the one you love. Seeing storefronts with cut-out cupids and "Be Mine" and "Yours Always" banners at the gas stations was enough to guilt even the most unfaithful man into taking the right exit off the parkway into residential suburbia, far away from our hotel.

I was hoping to get laid on Valentine's Day, which was a Saturday. My mother had dinner reservations for two at the local Italian place, Rizzuto's. She and my dad would be gone for at least an hour. That ought to be long enough.

I wondered if I'd be able last long enough.

I kept an extra copy to the key to Room 54, which was near the end of the even-numbered wing. How could I get Lee Anderson there? She'd started letting me feel her tits and ass in the teacher's lounge if we were alone, but she wouldn't touch my cock. I tried to press it against her hip, but she would just back up and giggle.

I was prepared, though. I had an emptied tissue box

under my bed filled with unused condoms I'd found in the rooms. There were lubricated, non-lubricated, and ribbed varieties. The ribbed ones were also lubricated. I also had those Venus beads and an unopened tin of orgy butter. Not that I was expecting an orgy. One girl was enough for now.

I knew you could get a girl pregnant the first time both of you had sex. One *Hustler* reader thought that if the girl douched right after with Coca-Cola, the sperm wouldn't be able to fertilize her eggs. How stupid.

Other kids weren't having *sex* sex, but there was this girl in the grade below, Nancy Kellogg, who gave blow jobs for five dollars. I heard she swallowed and everything. Lee even told me. When you saw Nancy waiting by the gym supply closet after school, you knew she was going to give a blow job. She was okay looking, with bangs of light blonde hair around her face, but her neck still had a collar of baby fat. Her body wasn't fat, and she was getting some nice tits, but that didn't really make up for it. I thought I could do better than her. Lee Anderson was the centerfold in my book. Nancy was just a girl you'd see in the hard-core mags.

I called Lee's house on the pay phone outside the closed hamburger stand. Her father answered.

"Hullo?"

"Hi, yes, may I speak with Lee?"

"Yeah, wait a sec." I could hear him yell, "Lee! Phone!"

"Hello?" asked Lee a few seconds later. She had

answered on another extension.

"Lee, it's me."

"Hey!" she said a little too loud and then immediately added a softer, "Hey." I heard the sharp click of her father hanging up his receiver.

"Are you going to be home on Valentine's Day?"

"Are you going to send me flowers?"

"No, nothing like that," I said, taken aback by her enthusiasm. Flowers? Never even thought of that. "No, I was thinking maybe you could come over or something."

"I can't, it's also my mother's birthday. I've got to be home all day."

"You can't sneak out around dinner or something, can you?"

"No, my uncles and aunts are coming and everything for dinner. It's a big thing. Maybe I could see you some other weekend, okay? At that hotel, right?"

"Yeah," I said, "yeah, some other weekend." Hope jettisoned out an open hatch and into the void, tumbling over and over through silent space. Valentine's Day was the only day I could be sure neither of my parents would be at home. Since I never had friends over, they sure as hell wouldn't understand why I'd bring a girl over. Or maybe they'd know all too well.

"See you in school," I said, feeling like a sucker. She made a kissing sound. "Okay," I said.

I thought about what it was like having one of those big family dinners, and whether Lee's mom and aunts were sexy or not. If they were, did they ever play around with each other?

The receiver started buzzing, and I became aware that I was still clutching it. I hung up and started the long walk back to the office. As I passed by the rooms, I thought about all the people who had fucked in them. My life was renting and cleaning those rooms, but there was no fucking for me. Just flipping the mattresses over.

Peter Fiorello was at the counter when I came in the office.

"Hey, look who's here!" Heartiness shook through his heavy frame. "Hey, why so down?"

"Nothing." I sauntered around the counter and sat down on the stool.

"I know you boys get moody when you're this age. My boys were always grumpy, talking back. You should enjoy it when you're young." Mrs. Fiorello stepped in, holding a large tweed suitcase in one hand and a shopping bag in the other.

"Was that you riding your bicycle by the highway?" she asked me.

"When?"

"Last week! That was you riding with only one hand! And Peter thought it was a Chinese food-delivery man! You're going to get in an accident! I should tell your mother."

"There's no Chinese delivery in this town," I said. "What's in the suitcase?"

"Oh, I've brought some presents for you and your mommy and daddy," she said. She dumped the shopping bag on the counter, spilling little Chinese trinkets and candies. Tiny paper lamps. Rice-paper candies. Haw flakes. Honey noodle cakes. Even firecrackers. All strewn across the counter. What was this cheap Chinese stuff doing here, out in front for any customer to see? For me to see? How was I supposed to rent out rooms with all this chinkiness on display? It was a mockery of my authority. Of my status as an American. I was horrified.

"I stopped at the oriental store!" Mrs. Fiorello said. "Happy Valentine's Day!"

"Is this any good?" asked Peter Fiorello, picking up a small packet of dried sour plums.

"You tell me," I said, backing out of the office and into the kitchen to get a glass of milk.

"Looks like a bunch of shrunken heads…" he muttered.

The next weekend, Peter Fiorello was dead from a heart attack. I got a phone call from his son because his family found a key from our hotel in Peter's vest pocket. They wanted to know if Peter had any stuff stored down here.

I found out that Peter and the woman we thought was Mrs. Fiorello weren't married. Peter's real wife had died five years before. He'd re-met his childhood sweetheart at the funeral. Peter's kids, who were in their 20s and living at home, hated the woman, so the two of them had decided to come down to New Jersey on the weekends to be alone. She became Mrs. Fiorello. And, of course, Fiorello wasn't his real name.

CHAPTER 15

In March, we jacked the room rates back up and the old men moved out to God knew where. I watched them pack their beat-up suitcases into the backs of their beat-up cars. They handed in their room keys at the office, standing and talking to my mother as she endured one last conversation with each of them.

I walked into the office and I saw her kiss Frank over the counter. It bothered the hell out of me, seeing her kiss this sprout of white hair and wrinkles. She and my father never kissed.

"Sorry to see you go, Frank," I said sarcastically.

"Jerk kid!"

"Frank's going to Los Angeles," my mother said.

"Hope you die on the way," I muttered as Frank limped out the door.

"Why did you kiss him!" I shouted as soon as he'd gone. My mother looked stunned, taken aback by her son yelling at her.

"He has cancer!" she said. "He lift his neck and show me all tumors on his throat. It look disgusting!"

"But why did you kiss him!" I yelled again. My anger

surprised me. This time, she frowned and waved her hand at me.

"Don't bother me! I work hard all day! Who buys clothes for you? Who buys food for you? You owe me everything! You stupid!" At that moment, I thought about my father. Where was he? In the workshop? Under the hotel?

I found him sitting on the steps at the entrance to the crawlspace. His left hand was wrapped in a wet towel.

"What happened?" I asked him.

"I thought pipe was cooled down, but it wasn't." He unwrapped the towel and showed me an angry red slash across his palm.

He shook his head and wrapped his hand up again.

"You know, ah, I just saw mom kiss a customer. In the office."

"That's part of business. Doesn't matter to me. Down here is where man's job is. I have to replace plumbing circuit. I have to replace all electrical wires. Then all floors have to be replaced."

"All of them?"

"All." He thought for a minute. "When you get older and help fix more things, it will be better."

For homework that night, I had to write a creative essay on how spring was coming in, like a lamb or like a lion. I said it was coming in like a lion because people were getting meaner.

At about 10 p.m., Lee Anderson called the hotel to talk to me. We only had that one phone line, and my parents were concerned about potential business lost, so they listened in on all my conversations with extreme scrutiny. There was no privacy in the living quarters and the phone cord only stretched from the end of the couch to behind the office desk.

"Tell me you love me," Lee said. She was talking on the extension in her own room. My parents would never understand paying for more than one phone per family.

"I love you," I mumbled quickly.

"You're only saying that because I told you to."

"No, I'm not."

"Do you always have to work on the weekend?"

"I have to work here every day. Weekends are the worst."

"I can come over there. My brother can drop me off."

"Hey, I gave you a chance. My parents are almost always here."

"So what?"

"We can't do anything."

"We can just hang out or something."

"There's nothing to do here."

"We could go see a movie. I want to see 'Psycho 2.'"

"I can't go anywhere. I have to help out here."

"Just for a few hours."

"I can't. I just can't."

"Are you ashamed of me or something? Am I not good enough for you?" she asked.

"It's my parents," I said, curling my entire body around the receiver to muffle as much sound as possible. "They're weird about some things…"

"They want you to have a Chinese girlfriend, right?"

"They don't want me to have any girlfriend at all. Not until college."

"That's weird."

"I know, they're really weird people."

"So you should tell them you love me."

"I don't even love *them*."

"Really?"

"Yeah, really. That sound funny to you?"

"Yeah, it does. But I'm sure they love you."

"Lee, Chinese people don't care about anybody else."

"You only want to fuck me."

"That's not true."

"All these older boys try to pick me up after school, but I tell them I have a boyfriend."

"Well, if I'm your boyfriend, shouldn't you fuck me?"

"You're not being very romantic," she said and hung up.

When I got into school the next day, I ripped out a piece of paper from my spiral notebook and wrote "LEE I LOVE YOU" on it inside a lopsided heart. I folded it twice and slipped it into the upper vent of her locker. The note was ugly and stupid, but it worked. Later that day, we hugged in a stairwell and I squeezed her ass. I wondered how long it would be before I got her in bed. Thinking about the hand job from Anne-Marie didn't even get me hard anymore. I had to go to the next level.

I was getting off the bus at the hotel one day when some kid leaned out the window and yelled, "Have a

Happy Easter!"

I yelled back, "Shut up, faggot!"

I got about halfway up the driveway when a big Fairlaine pulled up next to me. Roy leaned out of the driver's window and waved me over. I went over to him, but he said, "No, get in the car!"

I went around to the passenger's side and got in.

"What was that you yelled at the boy on the bus?" asked Roy, after I closed the door.

"I called him a faggot."

"Why did you call him a faggot?"

"Because he told me Happy Easter."

"Easter's about a month away."

"He was making a joke, because Chinese people have teeth like Easter bunnies."

"They do, don't they?" he said, smiling. "So anyway, I just wanted to say goodbye. I'm going."

"Yeah, sorry the room rates went back up."

"Oh, no, it's a good thing. This will get me on my way again. I don't want to get too comfortable anywhere."

"Where are you going to go?"

"Anywhere I want."

"Where's that?"

"You know, you got a speech problem. You always end everything with a question mark."

"Just asking."

"I packed everything into the car and checked out with your mother this morning. And then I waited in this car all afternoon just so I could say goodbye to you."

I was stunned. No one ever went out of their way to do

anything for me, let alone say goodbye.

"How come?"

"Because I worry about you, little man. You can't stand up for yourself in a snowball fight. You going around calling people faggots and talking about getting laid and everything. Just remember, if you have sex, wear a condom. I'm warning you."

"I thought you said sex complicates everything."

Roy heaved a heavy sigh. "You know, I left a son in Vietnam. His mother is a really wonderful woman. He's a few years younger than you. But I think about him when I see you."

"Does he look like me?"

"I haven't seen him in a while. His mother, too."

"Maybe you should bring them here."

"I've got a wife here."

"You're married?"

"In the process of getting unmarried. This is what I meant about things getting complicated..." He trailed off.

"Okay, well, I'll see you later, Roy," I said, putting a hand on the door latch.

"Wait, let me give you a ride down to the office."

"It's like a hundred feet away."

"Please, let me. Least I can do."

He drove me down to the office and watched me get out. Then his car turned slowly and he was gone.

With the spring thaw, the flow of johns came back to the hotel in full force. Ten to 15 pulled in and out a night.

"How much for a couple of hours?" asked one john.

"Twenty."

"It's worth it to get laid, isn't it?" he asked. Not getting a reply from me, he looked into my eyes and smiled. "Isn't it worth it?" he asked again.

"Yeah, sure it is," I said. When I cleaned out his room later. The bed hadn't been touched. It must have been one of those quickies on the floor. He left an unopened bottle of St. Pauli Girl in the bathtub, though. The label was wrinkled and peeling off. I wondered if getting drunk was like having sex.

I sat on the unmade bed and took my rubber gloves off, then opened the bottle and took a swig. It was warm and tasted lousy, like the bitter barley tea I once drank by accident when I found it in the fridge. Still, I drank the whole thing. I felt my face flush up. A rushing sound blocked out my hearing. I lay back on the dirty bed, waiting to feel something good, but it didn't even feel as good as jerking off. I fell asleep for about an hour on that hotel bed.

"Hey, you!" It was the head Benny on the phone.

"Hey, Vincent!"

"What's up there, you horny little bastard?"

"What's going on?"

"Yeah, well, I was wondering if you had, uh, if you could let me stay down there for a few days. I gotta get out of town, you know?"

"What?"

"Some guy's after me because I fucked his sister. I didn't force her, or nothing. She was drunk, I was drunk.

You understand, my man?"

"Yeah, I understand."

"I knew you would, that's why I'm glad I got you on the phone and not your parents. We got that between us. You're my best friend down there. You can just slip me a room key and not charge me, right? I'm a little short on the moolah right now."

"Well, I don't know about that," I said. My mother and father would blast through the roof like a two-stage space rocket if they knew I was giving a room away. "How long are you going to stay?"

"Just a couple of weeks. Gimme a room near the end so people don't see me coming in and out. I'm gonna be down there late on Friday night. The car's in the shop, so I'm gonna take the train down."

"Okay," I said, just then realizing that he'd talked his way into getting a free room.

But Vincent never showed up that Friday night. I was sitting behind the desk, reading "A Modest Proposal" in my school literature book, when the police came in. There were two of them. One was tall and gaunt and kept his hands in his pockets. The other had a broken nose and a wide frame. They both looked sleepy and shuffled around the office like they were looking for a place to lie down.

"Hey kid, you got a Vincent Bruno staying here?" asked the gaunt cop.

"No," I said quickly, feeling my heart race. I was having flashbacks to the other cop who'd stopped by.

"Can I get a look at the registration cards?" I handed them over, even though I knew the police were supposed to have a search warrant to see them. Gaunt Cop flipped through the cards, holding them at an angle so Broken Nose could see them, too. Broken Nose shook his head at each card.

"Okay, thanks," said Gaunt Cop, handing the cards back. "He stays here in the summer, right?"

"Yes," I said, suddenly feeling like I'd just betrayed Vincent, the only person who would play Atari with me. "What did he do?" The cops looked at each other.

"Scumbag's a rapist," Broken Nose said, ending his sentence with a loud yawn.

"Oh," I said.

"Kid like you shouldn't be working here," Broken Nose said, looking around at the far corners of the office ceiling.

"My parents own this place."

"That's real good," Broken Nose said, smirking and glancing at Gaunt Cop. "That's real good," he said again.

"If this guy shows up, give us a call. We'll be back," Gaunt Cop said, ignoring Broken Nose's comments.

"I'm not fucking around," said Broken Nose. "You pick up that phone and call when you see him." The office door closed with a sharp click behind them. I watched their car pull out to see if they would flash their red and blue lights, but they didn't.

Half an hour later, I was renting out another room to a john.

CHAPTER 16

It wasn't until the end of April that Lee Anderson touched my hard-on with her hands. She would let me push it against her pussy or her hip, but then I got behind her in the teacher's lounge. I pushed it between her ass cheeks, which were well-defined in those tight Gloria Vanderbilt jeans.

"Oh!" she yelped, turning and kissing me. She put her arms around my waist, but I grabbed her left hand and put it on my cock. "Gee, that's pretty hard," she said.

"Rub it," I said. She giggled and withdrew. "I wish you could blow me here."

"What!"

"I've never had a blow job," I said.

"I've never given one," she said.

"Always a first time."

"Maybe we should go to college together, then we could live in the same apartment. My sister does that with her boyfriend." Then her voice faltered. "You know, I'm moving in the summer."

"To where?" I asked, shocked.

"California." In a soft voice she added, "My dad lost

his job. We're going to move in with my uncle."

"God...California..."

"We could meet again in college. We'll go to the same place. We could cook together, too. Wouldn't that be fun? I love cooking."

"What about...you know?"

"I know..." she said.

"Well, how about before you leave?" I asked.

"I don't want to...I need to watch my reputation." She sighed. "I think you're the cutest thing and of course I love you. You know, I just need some more time." I placed a hand on each of her breasts.

"I think you're the perfect girl," I told her. She blushed. "Really?"

"Yes," I said, squeezing her tits. "Really." Two more months and she'd be in California. I only had two more months.

Memorial Day weekend was a few weeks away, which meant it was time to tidy up the doorstep and shake out the rugs for the return of the Bennys.

I was killing time between errands at the hardware store and buying groceries, and as I walked down to the end of the boardwalk and back, I inhaled deeply. It smelled like salt and booze.

Tractors on the beach dragged what looked like huge rakes across the sands, clearing away planks of driftwood, garbage, and dead horseshoe crabs that had washed up during the stormy spring months. Crews hammered new planks onto the boardwalk. Watching them work made me think of Mitchell Cone's father.

The boardwalk stands had reopened, and newly hired barkers would practice the patter that would lure Benny men into their stalls to buy softballs and break plates. Two-foot high stuffed Smurfs formed a first line of defense around the stands. Smaller Smurfs and fake animals covered the back walls. They tricked you into thinking you could win the big Smurfs with one fifty-cent try, but you had to win five times – break 15 plates – to get one. With only one win, you'd never get more than a keychain. All the stands had their sucker angle. The water gun relays, the go-fish pond, the rubber frog leap, and the no-frills quarter toss. You could never get the best prize with only one shot, no matter how good you were.

"Haw! Haw! Haw!" screeched the seagulls.

When I got to the supermarket, I saw that they'd already stacked Styrofoam coolers to the ceiling. They loomed like monoliths from a primitive culture. Bags of ice pushed the popsicles and ice cream down into a lone shelf in the freezer. It was going to be another big summer, a real scorcher. Even the gas stations were stocking suntan lotion. Another season to make money.

The big three-day Memorial Day weekend was getting closer. "Everybody's Working for the Weekend," by Loverboy was getting heavy airplay. We reopened the entire hotel. Rooms that had been shut all winter and spring had to be aired out.

I walked from room to room with an ice bucket filled with keys and a clipboard. I checked the keys to each room, marking down if there were one or two beds in it and making sure the television worked. If a room smelled funny, I would close the toilet lid, stand on it, and crack open the bathroom window.

Then it was here. You could feel the buzz of leased Pontiacs driving south from the city. All the rooms were gone by 8 p.m. on Friday, even at our inflated prices. Friday and Saturday night were $50 each, but if you took Friday, Saturday, and Sunday night, you only had to pay $40 per night.

Two women signing in for a room asked me if there were a lot of singles in town.

I said I didn't know. They were both nearly blind drunk and had stumbled into the office out of their car, leaving the doors open and the headlights on. One had a flabby face that she tried to diminish with mounds of teased brown hair. The other was a cute blonde with black eyebrows. That meant her pussy hair was black, too.

"Are you single?" asked the flabby one while the blonde giggled. "I was thinking maybe we could we do something about the price? Maybe we could find some way to lower it."

"I'm sorry, I can't go any lower," I said.

"I mean I could go lower. You know? I mean all the way down," said the flabby one. "Both of us would," she said, her pointed finger spinning in the air. She looked anxious.

This was *Love Letters* material. It wasn't the first time I'd been offered sex, but it was the first time it had happened with girls I'd take the offer up with. Two drunk women giving me head at the same time, passing it back and forth between them.

But something was wrong. The blonde was shaking her head.

"I don't wanna...Chinaman! They got small dicks. Jesus, small dicks!" she whined. A look of alarm washed over the flabby woman's face.

"She's drunk, already, she won't even care! She doesn't care!" she said. But it killed the moment for me. The blonde was the one I really wanted.

"That's $127.20 for the three days, with the tax," I said. Their American Express card didn't go through, but the flabby girl handed me a Visa card that was approved. I scrawled the acceptance number on the form. I got the signature from the flabby girl while the blonde frowned.

"You can't sign for my card," she said.

"I just did," said the flabby girl. The signature was close enough, and I gave her the receipt and the carbons.

My mother had tried to call Nancy to ask if she could come back to clean rooms, but the number didn't work anymore. My mother ended up hiring two high-school girls. On Monday, she started training the girls how to clean rooms. By then, most of the rooms had checked out already, though some Bennys were still hanging out in the parking lot, sitting on their car bumpers and trying to finish the rest of their beer before hitting the road.

My mother left the two girls on the odd-numbered wing and went back to the front desk. The maid's cart was fully packed with the vacuum cleaner and massive amounts of toilet paper, soap, and towels. Its swivel wheels were stuck in four different directions. The girls struggled to push the cart down to the next room, but the wheels were jammed. They rocked the cart back and forth like a stubborn, overloaded mule.

I was busy with hauling out cases of Howdy! and Briardale Cola, so I didn't take any further notice of their lack of progress. If the girls weren't so unfuckable, I might have paid them more attention. Both were wearing t-shirts and shorts, and didn't have bodies that deserved to show any more. If I'd run across their pictures in a magazine, I would have flipped to the next pictorial.

A short while later, I heard a few splashes in the pool. It was about 4 p.m., a few hours after check-out time, but I didn't care if people went for a swim before actually leaving. I locked up the newly stocked soda machines and headed back for the office, passing by the pool. I saw four wet mounds of hair at the edge of the shallow end. Little ripples radiated out from the lightly bobbing heads. The Bennys were humping the maids in the water. The cart was still outside of Room 41, which meant the girls had cleaned one room in the past hour. My mother was going to flip.

As I approached the office door, she was already charging out to the swimming pool with the cordless phone in hand. She had seen the girls jump into the pool from her perch on the office bar stool. The cordless phone wouldn't work from that far away, but its physical presence and the threat to call the police on the two Bennys who were rubbing up against 15-year-olds would be enough to break up this pool party. I couldn't hear what was going on down there, but watching the four bodies scramble out of the pool was enough to make me wish I had the balls to just grab a girl and fuck her.

Later on that afternoon, I went around the hotel with a new pair of giant Craftsman shears. The evergreen bushes that had been planted across the arms of the hotel had grown out unevenly. The builder had intended for the bushes to line the inside driveway, like velvet in a jewel case, but most of the bushes had died, leaving withered stumps that drunk customers stumbled over.

I cut into the overgrown bushes, trying to make them look like rectangles or round globs, depending on how dense the branches were. I was tired after the fourth one, and my arms ached like I'd pitched extra innings. But I did find a water-damaged and sun-dried issue of *Gallery* nestled in a pile of dead needles. The pages were warped, and some were stuck together, but I managed to get one pictorial opened – two women alternating on a pool table, with cue sticks. The pictures were discolored, and their skin had been stained brown. The next page I was able to rip open had the right colors.

After staring at some pussy, I tore into the rest of the bushes with lust-driven abandon. I thought about fucking Lee Anderson on that pool table. Chop. Chop. Chop. When I was done, I swept the cuttings into plastic garbage bags and dumped them in the woods. My upper arms and shoulder blades hurt all night.

On my way out to the bus the next day, I grabbed the

key to Room 54. I had a Trojan ribbed condom in my jacket pocket. I was thinking about bringing the cock ring, but I'd never tried it, and I didn't want to risk anything going wrong. I'd been jerking off so much anyway that I thought I'd be able to last long enough on my own.

In the teacher's lounge, I stuck my hand into Lee Anderson's left back pocket. My thumb was on her panty line.

"Come back on my bus with me," I whispered into her ear.

"What for?" she asked.

"It's a surprise."

"What kind of surprise?" I forced myself into her belt buckle and she frowned, but didn't back away.

"Is that all you want?" she asked. I shook my head.

"I want some of this, too," I said, sweeping my free hand across the side of her breast.

"I…I don't know," Lee began, trying to maneuver away, but my hand on her ass kept her from breaking free.

"I mean, you love me, don't you? You said you loved me, Lee."

"I do."

"Then come back with me, if you really love me."

"I don't want to do it, you know? Not yet."

"If you love me, you will," I said. "If you really love me, you will."

I held her hand on the bus. When we got on, I was afraid that Mrs. Krackowski was going to demand a bus pass or permission slip for Lee. But the old woman just winked and said, "So, you're taking a little friend home! She's cute, she your girlfriend?" We didn't say anything.

Lee's hand was sweaty and slippery. I could smell the salt in her palm. I sat by the window and kept watch for the familiar landmarks. The car wash. The pancake house. The gas station. I wanted to make sure this bus wasn't going off-course. Nothing was going to stop me from fucking this girl.

I suddenly realized that I hadn't looked into Lee's face since we sat down. I turned to her and brought my knee up on the seat between us without letting go of her hand. Her eyes were half-closed, but when I ducked my head to see under her eyelids, I saw her pupils rattling back and forth like beautiful blue marbles in a glass tumbler.

"I love you, Lee," I said.

"I'm scared," she said.

"Don't be," I said. "It's natural."

When we got off, I snuck her off to the side to hide from my mother's view if she was waiting in the office. We prowled up to the even-numbered wing of the hotel. Cars passing on the highway must have wondered what those two sneaking kids were up to. I looked down and was surprised to see that I was still holding Lee's hand. I put my arm around her waist, and we made a dash for Room 54.

The first thing we did when the door was shut and the shades were drawn was laugh. We laughed like we had just stepped off a death-defying carnival ride and were walking off the platform.

It was dark, but I could tell the place hadn't been cleaned. I smelled the beer and cigarette smoke. A thin strap of light from the window sliced through the room and lit up the neck of an opened beer bottle on the desk.

Being in that dirty room with a girl felt strange. I had a sudden impulse to sweep the pillows to the floor, pull off the sheets from the four corners and fuck her on that bare comestained mattress.

I felt for the edge of the bed and sat down on it, pulling Lee's ass onto my lap. I kissed her over her shoulder as I fumbled with her belt.

"It's a magnet," she tried to say as my lips squeezed hers like a vice with rubber grips. Her jeans split open. Then they were around her ankles, and my fingers were rubbing what felt like a big eyebrow.

I turned and dropped her on the unmade bed. I stepped on the inner sole of each of my shoes and pried them off. My clothes slumped to the floor as I undressed quickly, shirt and jeans slipping off like butter on a hot biscuit.

Vincent told me women liked to pretend to hate sucking cock, but they expected to have to, anyway. They had to pretend so you wouldn't think they were sluts. I had my hands delicately wrapped around Lee's ears. I pulled a little. After a moment of uncertainty, it was in her mouth. I held my breath the whole time.

Then it was my turn to suck. I thought pussy would smell and taste bad, but I couldn't smell or taste anything. Lee had taken off her blouse and bra. Her nipples were hard, and I teethed them.

I ripped the foil and rolled the condom down until I felt a cold ring of rubber and lubricant at my balls. I'd practiced jerking off with the condom and lubricant in my hands lots of times.

I crawled on top of Lee and pushed her thighs out. I felt less resistance than I thought there'd be. My body shook. By the sound she was making, I could tell her teeth were gritted, and I could feel her spit on my throat. I felt my muscles tighten, and then I came. I'd lasted about a minute.

The penis-pump ads said premature ejaculation was anything less than five minutes. What was wrong with me? It took more than 15 minutes for me to jerk off when I was trying not to come. Maybe I would always come early when fucking for real. This was terrible.

I got up and stumbled to the bathroom on shaky legs. I tugged at the condom, and it slipped off into my hand. When my bare feet hit the cold tile, I hit the light switch.

I'd heard about the blood that came from a popped cherry, but I didn't know how much to expect. In the pus-yellow light, my balls were drenched in impossibly dark red. Blood streaked down my legs. The condom in my right hand looked like cellophane wrap that had been pulled off of fresh roast beef. A rhombus of light from the bathroom made a crooked frame around Lee's body from the neck on down. She was rubbing her legs but didn't make a sound. The blood against her white skin stood out in higher contrast than on mine. Her eyes shone in the dark, and she was looking up at the ceiling.

She might have been crying.

I'd never seen any pictures with blood smeared around, just come.

I pissed on the floor. I couldn't move my feet.

CHAPTER 17

I was tired as hell the next day in school. I'd gone into school after cleaning rooms all night before, but I had never been this tired. My entire body ached, even my ass muscles. I must've looked like I was a druggie. But Lee looked fine. As if nothing had happened.

I'd called Seaside Taxi from the pay phone to take her home, then waited right by the highway with her, watching the sky darken to a deep blue and lights leaking from passing cars. I gave her five dollars and a small hug before she got in and left.

Something was different now for us in school. Lee wanted to hold hands all the time. It was fun for a few days. Then it got embarrassing. Then one day she was out sick.

"You get Lee pregnant, or something?" Crispy asked me.

"Naw…" I said. I'd been careful every time.

"You did fuck her."

"Might have," I said, feeling a sliver of pride. "So when are you gonna be balling, Queer Bait Crispy?" I asked, punching him in the shoulder as hard as I could.

Something slammed against the blackboard.

"No talking!" Mr. Hendrickson yelled before continuing our review session. "A lot of you are asking me about the final exam even though it's still a few weeks away," he continued, kicking away broken chalk. "I haven't even made a goddamn outline yet, so get off my fucking back, already." As the school year drew to a close, Hendrickson's dual persona had merged until he was launching into violent curses even when his glasses were on.

I cared less and less about school. One day, I realized I had nothing to write with. I stuck a hand into the back of my desk. All I found was a stubby pencil. I tried to erase with it, but the metal eraser clip was empty, and I ended up ripping a slash in my notebook.

We fucked a whole bunch of times. In Room 54, and a few times in the woods on an old blanket.

I threw all my magazines into a Hefty bag and dumped them with the bush clippings in the woods. I didn't need them anymore. I had the perfect girl.

In the second week of June, a dizzying heat wave clamped down, slowing down my thoughts and movements. They let us wear shorts in school, and I shivered when the backs of my thighs touched the cold molded plastic of our seats.

I had just gotten back to the classroom from gym. I was early because I wore the same shorts in gym that I did around school and didn't need to change. Mr. Hendrickson came over to me.

"Your daddy's been in an accident," he said. "Mrs. Daly will give you a ride to the hospital." Mrs. Daly was the principal's secretary, a bitter, crusty old widow. I had been terrified of her since my second-grade class had elected me to bring the absentee slips to the principal's office. Mrs. Daly's sharp eyes would narrow as she snatched the slips out of my hand.

Mrs. Daly's Duster was a shrine on four wheels. It was loaded with small boardwalk teddy bears and other dolls that crowded each other in the back seats and tumbled over the dashboard. Three poseable plastic figures hung from the stem of the rear-view mirror as if they'd been lynched. With the bears, the dolls, and the searing heat in the car, there wasn't much room for air. It reminded me of a picture I'd seen of a Chinese temple with thousands of carved images of Buddha repeated on every surface. Rows and rows of smiling faces and rounded heads and bellies.

"I am so sorry," said Mrs. Daly. "I heard what happened. You have my sympathies." She sounded sincere, but her expression still had a sharp edge that could slice apples through the core. I didn't know what she was sorry for, though, because no one had told me any details yet.

I signed in at the hospital desk and rode the elevator to the fourth floor. My sneakers squeaked against the polished floor like I was walking across a giant, empty basketball court. I never felt as small as I did when I walked into that room and saw the white curtain pulled around my father's tired form under the sheets. His limp face was pale and rippled.

I didn't yet know what a stroke was, but my father had had one. My mother had found him in the basement trying to pull himself up off the floor. He'd been screaming for hours, but I was at school, and my mother had been out cleaning rooms.

His left side was paralyzed, probably permanently. If any movement was going to come back, we'd know in the next few days.

And then we knew.

I was excused from the rest of school, all two weeks of it, and I spent those days behind the counter and cleaning rooms, playing tag team with my mother. No finals for me, but no Lee Anderson, either. She called a few times, saying over and over that she was sorry about my dad, that she loved me, and that she was moving real soon, in that order. She made me take down her address and phone number twice the day she was leaving. This time, when she made the kissy sounds, I made them, too. It was okay because no one was listening.

My mother and I could never be in the same place at the same time because we couldn't rent rooms if they weren't clean, and we also couldn't rent rooms without someone in the office. My father's absence began to take its toll on the business. We had to cross two rooms off our sheets because the hot water wouldn't turn off in one and the other didn't get any water at all. I'd gone into the crawlspace and turned a few knobs, but I didn't know what I was doing, and nothing had happened.

One day, I found my mother sitting on the office couch

with her head in her hands, rocking back and forth. She wouldn't say anything. I thought she might be having a stroke, too.

"Are you okay? Hey!"

She took her hands away from her face and covered her ears.

My father's medical bills for just the first few weeks had sunk our savings. We had no health insurance. Why should we? He was young. We were all young. Who knew you could have a stroke at 42?

The hospital worked out an installment plan for the rest, but we weren't going to make it, even if the rooms were full every day. And we still had monthly mortgage payments on the hotel.

Everybody was going to come down on us. The laundry service would cut us off. Then the cleaning-supplies company, the phone company, the electric and gas companies. The bank would repossess our stuff. Even the Pinto.

I woke up once in the middle of the night because I heard shouting. But it had been me yelling in my sleep.

There were calls to Taiwan. There were calls from Taiwan. I was sleepwalking to hotel rooms with a bucket in each hand. I put sanitized bands around toilet seats without even cleaning them. In the sunlight, the Bennys moved awkwardly and carefree, bouncing spinning Frisbees off of their toes and onto the beer bottles they were holding. There were a few barbecues on the lawn. I wanted to see those Frisbees turn into circular saw blades and lop heads off. I wanted to see headless bodies charbroil on the grill.

I thought of my father in the rehabilitation wing, half of his face and one shoulder and hip slumped down as he struggled with a walker. He was literally a broken man.

My father had given his life to the Bennys. Next on the menu were me and my mom.

I dropped my cleaning buckets and went behind the odd-numbered wing of the hotel. I was trying to breathe two inhales ahead of what I could, and I fell on my knees. I was so tired, it felt like too much work to lie down.

My eyesight was going. I heard blood rushing past my ears. I looked up. Somewhere, high above, the sun was shining. But I couldn't see it.

I didn't play Atari or even watch television anymore. I barely had time to brush my teeth before falling over asleep.

One night, when I was cleaning rooms by myself, I went into the supply closet to get more toilet bands and saw the rocket-shaped rear reflector of my bicycle poking out from behind a wall of towels. I pulled my bike out and wiped it down. It still looked like it was in good shape.

I went around the hotel, nice and easy. The moon was out, pouring a watery gleam over the handles as I made the turns. It was effortless. I couldn't feel my legs or my arms, just the sensation of a slow coast downhill.

Then I felt something give under my right leg. I looked down and saw the pedal coming loose. It fell off, and I hopped off and picked it up. The grooves around the mouth of the cylinder had been eaten away so I couldn't reattach it.

"Motherfucking whore slut!" I yelled at the bike. I kicked it in the spokes, then dragged it back home. I stood at the top of the stairs leading down to the basement and gave it a push from the seat. The bike bucked like a pissed-off horse in a rodeo as it tumbled down.

The next day I tried calling Lee at her new number in California.

"This is Paul Tee Real Estate," said a man with a cheery voice.

"Hello? Is Lee Anderson there?" I asked, looking again at the number I had written down and running my finger under it. I heard a heavy sigh.

"Lee Anderson, you mean my little niece?"

"You're her uncle?"

"Don't get fucking wise with me!" the man sneered. "I don't need to be taking phone calls for my fucking niece!"

"Is she there?"

"Why does this run in my goddamn wife's family? Why do they have kids when they can't hold a job because they drink all the time? Now they're giving the phone number out like it's their phone? Who pays the goddamn phone bill?

"I don't have enough problems, already? I'm trying to feed my wife and our kids and we have to take in her fucking older brother and his family? I'm taking messages for my stupid niece when I'm trying to run a business out of this house? I need people sleeping in my basement?" He was shouting so loud, I could hear his voice in the ear that wasn't next to the receiver.

"I'm paying for the phone call. I just want to talk to Lee…"

"And I just want to live without people hanging on my back! Why do you people have three kids when you can't pay down your mortgage? Why buy new color TVs when you know you can't afford the credit-card payments? Don't you people ever think of saving money? Is there no shame in leeching off of relatives? I've been working since I was 10 fucking years old! No one ever gave me shit!" He slammed down the phone so hard I thought I heard the receiver crack.

I woke up in the middle of the night again. It was becoming a bad habit. My stomach hurt so much, I put my hand over it and rolled out of bed onto the floor. What was wrong? I hadn't jerked off in more than a month. Maybe that was it.

I lay on the floor and stared at the moon. Something was jabbing me in the back, but I didn't know if it was a book or a shoe. Something else was pulling me up and away. Light from the moon and stars was shining on my doorknob. I got up and pulled on some jeans.

The next thing I knew, I was walking along the highway. I couldn't remember if I'd locked the office door or not. Clumps of rags and dented hubcaps littered my path. Sometimes a car would go by. The moon was pulling me to the beach.

I stepped up onto the ramp that led up to the board-walk. Hearing the sound of my feet on the boardwalk made it seem like the rest of the world was dead. The ocean was pitch black, but I could hear it slithering along the shoreline in the background.

Then I saw the beach. The craters and dunes looked like a lunar landscape. I'd finally gotten my wish. I was an astronaut on the moon. I was going to be famous and get a big promotion at NASA.

I jumped and ran all over the beach, spinning in circles and doing long jumps. Sand was getting into my shoes. I pranced around and screamed. Threw my head back and yelled and shook my fist at the stars. How many millions of years did it take for their light to reach the earth? How many of those stars were already dead and useless?

I lay down in the sand and looked up. I wasn't on the moon. Looking up in the sky, I could now see that I wasn't any closer to it than I'd ever been. I wasn't any closer to being an astronaut, and I wasn't any farther away from the hotel.

I felt my heart swell with hate. Hate for women. Hate for men. Hate for my mother, my father. Hate for sex.

I could fuck Lee in a hotel room or in the woods, but could I ever have sex in a bed, in a house, in a home?

I was crying now. Not the sobbing kind, but the kind where you feel lousy and then you notice tears rolling down. I flipped onto my stomach and crawled up the beach, away from the ocean.

I felt like a giant sea turtle in a science-class film, flailing in the sand, struggling to get far enough away from high tide to make a nest and lay eggs that I could never turn my neck far enough to see.

I kept crawling until I was under the boardwalk. It smelled like piss and booze down there. Cracks of dim light shone through the boards above me. I was still crying, and my eyes were blurry.

I saw a lot of scary things under there.

First I saw Vincent fucking me. And then I was fucking Vincent. Then it wasn't Vincent. It was my father. And then it was me.

I was ready to die. If I'd been a girl, I think I would have killed myself already. A girl renting out rooms at the hotel would have been raped before she was 11 or so. Gang-raped by drunk Bennys. Right in the office. My father wouldn't hear from the basement, and my mother would be out cleaning rooms.

Thank God I wasn't a girl. I howled with laughter. I couldn't remember the last time I'd thought, "Thank God."

I found a univalve seashell by one of the columns, and I put it up to my ear. I wanted to hear the ocean, but it sounded like some little boy laughing at me.

Two days later, I was riding with my mother to the airport in Newark. When I leaned my head against the window pane, I could feel the vibrations behind my eyeballs.

My father's older sister's family was coming to take over the hotel. They were going to get the living quarters, and we were going to live in Room 3, which was a nice room. My father was going to be in rehabilitation for another few months or so, but he was going to stay in

Room 3, too.

My mother and I were going to teach the family the business and help with their English. God knew what my father was going to do around the hotel. There was no way he was ever going to make it down the stairs to the workshop again.

My grandparents in Taiwan, my father's parents, were paying the mortgage. They said they'd take care of my college costs, too, as long as I worked at the hotel at night.

I met my cousins by the baggage claim. Suitcases moved around on the winding conveyor belt like slow slot-cars on a track.

The boy was about my age. The girl was a year or two younger.

I climbed into the back of the station wagon with the suitcases as the boy, the girl, and the mother fell asleep in the back seat. The father sat in the front talking with my mother. They nodded their heads a lot.

It was cramped where I was sitting, and my back was already sore from having boxed up most of our stuff and piling it into the attic. What we needed most was already in our hotel room – some clothes and some pans, bowls and spoons to go with our hotplate and tiny fridge.

Our relatives really wanted my mother and me to eat dinner with them, so we pulled into the Chinese place off the exit. It was a nice offer, since cooking anything beyond macaroni and cheese was a stretch in our hotel room.

"Make sure we buy enough for your father," said the man my mother had told me to call Uncle.

"Have to buy him sweet-and-sour pork," said my mother, pointing to me. "He doesn't eat anything Chinese."

"What!" Uncle said.

While we waited for our food to cook, the guy at the counter talked on the phone, with his back to us. Once in a while, he'd look over his shoulder at us and frown.

"What's wrong?" I asked my mother.

"They don't like people from Taiwan," she whispered. "They from Hong Kong."

Back at the hotel, I helped Uncle carry in the heavy suitcases.

"Strong! Very strong!" he said. Then I helped him carry some boxes down into the basement. I picked up my bike from the bottom of the stairs to clear a path. The little boy followed us down, gawking like he'd never seen a basement before. Uncle rubbed the baseball cap on the boy's head and said something in Chinese. We went back up.

"Aunty" set our old table quickly and opened every carton. The smell of all that Chinese food made me sick. She put the sweet-and-sour pork in front of me and smiled.

The two kids were sitting down already. They didn't make a sound. They looked like aliens, with skin much darker than mine. The boy took off his cap and I saw that his hair was shaved close to the scalp. The girl's hair was down to her chin, and it was thick and greasy and stuck to her cheeks.

My mother told me their names, but I was so mad at them, I couldn't hear her. These assholes were moving in, forcing us to live in a hotel room.

The kids were so tired, they left the kitchen without eating and slept on the sofa.

When dinner was over, my mother got together some rice and tofu for my father to eat back in the hotel room.

"You stay here. Watch office tonight," she told me. I was tired, but happy to still have an important position.

I told Uncle and Aunty to go to sleep. It was a pretty slow night. I only rented about three rooms. Around 5 a.m., I closed up the office. I figured my mother would come in around seven or so.

As I came in, my mother turned on her side and put her arm over my father. I'd never seen them that close before. It made me glad that I had my own bed, even though it was just a flimsy cot.

I was almost asleep when I heard a familiar sound from the hotel driveway.

No, it couldn't be, I thought. I put on a pair of sweat-pants and slipped outside to investigate.

The boy was on my bike, riding around the driveway. He was barefoot, with one foot on the left pedal and the other awkwardly on the shaft where the right pedal had been.

It wasn't night anymore, and it wasn't yet day. There weren't any shadows on the ground. The boy was wearing a bright white t-shirt and a pair of navy shorts. His dark legs were surprisingly muscular. He was beautiful.

I sat down on the step in the doorway and watched him go.

How long would it be before something terrible happened, I wondered. Lightning could strike him right now. He could hit a rock and go flying. Or maybe a parked car could back up into him.

But then I thought about that little boy pushing that broken bike all the way up the stairs from the basement. He must have wanted to ride that bike pretty bad.

Maybe life would be okay for that boy. After all, he had a sister. That was one more set of hands to help. He also had me.

The boy passed by, and I saw that his ankle had scraped against the bike chain and was bleeding. He smiled and waved to me while holding the bike steady. He was sitting back in the seat, pedaling slow like he was the only one in the race and all he had to do was finish.

I got up and got a soda from the machine. I drank some and shivered.

Then he came over, and I let him have some, too.